Praise for

Maybe He Just Likes You

"Mila is a finely drawn, sympathetic character dealing
with a problem all too common in middle school.
Readers will be cheering when she takes control! An
important topic addressed in an age-appropriate way."
**—Kimberly Brubaker Bradley, author of
Newbery Honor Book *The War That Saved My Life***

"In *Maybe He Just Likes You*, Barbara Dee sensitively
breaks down the nuances of a situation all too common
in our culture—a girl not only being harassed, but
not being listened to as she tries to ask for help. This
well-crafted story validates Mila's anger, confusion, and
fear, but also illuminates a pathway towards speaking up
and speaking out. A vital read for both girls and boys."
**—Veera Hiranandani, author of
Newbery Honor Book *The Night Diary***

"Mila's journey will resonate with many readers,
exploring a formative and common experience of
early adolescence that has too often been ignored.
Important and empowering."
**—Ashley Herring Blake, author of
Stonewall Children's & Young Adult Honor Book
*Ivy Aberdeen's Letter to the World***

"*Maybe He Just Likes You* is an important, timeless story
with funny, believable characters. Mila's situation is one
that many readers will connect with. This book is sure to
spark many productive conversations."
**—Dusti Bowling, author of
*Insignificant Events in the Life of a Cactus***

"In this masterful, relatable, and wholly unique
story, Dee shows how one girl named Mila finds
empowerment, strength, and courage within.
I loved this book."
—Elly Swartz, author of _Smart Cookie_ and _Give and Take_

"_Maybe He Just Likes You_ is the
perfect way to jump-start dialogue between
boy and girl readers about respect and boundaries.
This book is so good. So needed! I loved it!"
—Paula Chase, author of _So Done_ and _Dough Boys_

Praise for
Everything I Know About You

"[Tally's] passionate impulse to protect
her friends is immediately sympathetic, as is
her growing understanding of both herself
and her classmates. . . . A poignant and often
hilarious slice of middle-grade life."
—_Kirkus Reviews_

"Dee (_Star-Crossed_) sensitively portrays
Tally's fears about being left behind as friends
change, as well as the signs and impact of
the anorexia Ava is hiding. Readers will
root for big-hearted Tally, whose willingness
to speak her truth makes for honest and
engaging narration."
—_Publishers Weekly_

★ "A powerful story about surviving and thriving after serious illness."
—*SLJ*, starred review

"The authenticity of Norah's story can be credited to the author's own experiences as the mother of a cancer patient. But this is not a book about cancer; rather, it's about the process of moving forward in its wake. Readers who appreciate well-wrought portrayals of transformative middle-school experiences, such as Rebecca Stead's *Goodbye Stranger* (2015), will find a story in a similar spirit here."
—*Booklist*

"In writing this remarkable novel, Barbara Dee has performed an amazing feat. She has traveled to places you hope you will never have to go and then drawn a lovely, heartbreaking, warm, funny, and ultimately hopeful map of the way back home."
—Jordan Sonnenblick, author of *Drums, Girls, and Dangerous Pie*

"Barbara Dee has an unfailing sense of the dynamics of middle school social life. Spot-on portrayals of friends and family relationships frame a powerful main character who's determined to find her way back. *Halfway Normal* has a brave, kind heart—as tender and triumphant as the main character herself."
—Karen Romano Young, author of *Hundred Percent*

"Dee realistically explores the varied emotions of maturing middle-school students, as well as the way Norah feels singled out and patronized by classmates and adults alike."
—*Publishers Weekly*

Praise for
Star-Crossed

"A sweet story of young love amid middle school
theatrics . . . Readers cannot help but root for Mattie as she discovers
bravery she never gave herself credit for, both onstage and in life."
—Kirkus Reviews

"A sweet coming-out story for junior high readers. The clever
Shakespeare content is a bonus. . . . Verdict: A fine choice
for middle school libraries in need of accessible LGBTQ
stories, and a great option for students reading or performing
Romeo and Juliet."
—SLJ

"In this welcome addition to the middle grade LGBTQ
bookshelf . . . Dee (*Truth or Dare*) thoughtfully
dramatizes the intricate social performance of middle school,
with its secret crushes and fierce rivalries."
—Publishers Weekly

ALSO BY BARBARA DEE

MAYBE HE JUST LIKES YOU

BARBARA DEE

Aladdin

New York London Toronto Sydney New Delhi

ALADDIN

An imprint of Simon & Schuster Children's Publishing Division

1230 Avenue of the Americas, New York, New York 10020

First Aladdin hardcover edition October 2019

Text copyright © 2019 by Barbara Dee

Jacket illustration copyright © 2019 by Erika Pajarillo

For information about special discounts for bulk purchases, please contact Simon & Schuster Special Sales at 1-866-506-1949 or business@simonandschuster.com.

The Simon & Schuster Speakers Bureau can bring authors to your live event. For more information or to book an event contact the Simon & Schuster Speakers Bureau at 1-866-248-3049 or visit our website at www.simonspeakers.com.

Designed by Heather Palisi

The text of this book was set in Neutraface Slab.

Manufactured in the United States of America 0420BVG

4 6 8 10 9 7 5

Library of Congress Cataloging-in-Publication Data

Names: Dee, Barbara, author.

Title: Maybe he just likes you / by Barbara Dee.

Description: First Aladdin hardcover edition. | New York : Aladdin, 2019. |

Summary: When boys in her class start touching seventh-grader Mila and making her feel uncomfortable, she does not want to tell her friends or mother until she reaches her breaking point.

Identifiers: LCCN 2018048854 (print) | LCCN 2018053097 (eBook) |

ISBN 9781534432390 (eBook) | ISBN 9781534432376 (hc)

Subjects: | CYAC: Sexual harassment—Fiction. | Middle schools—Fiction. | Schools—Fiction. | Best friends—Fiction. | Friendship—Fiction. | Single-parent families—Fiction. | Family life—Fiction.

Classification: LCC PZ7.D35867 (eBook) | LCC PZ7.D35867 May 2019 (print) |

DDC [Fic]—dc23

LC record available at https://lccn.loc.gov/2018048854

For my son Josh
Proud of you in every way

MAYBE HE JUST LIKES YOU

PEBBLES

Every day that September, the four of us escaped out-doors. The weather was warm (a little too warm for fall, if you thought about it), and the cafeteria smelled gross, like melted cheddar cheese and disinfectant. So when the bell rang for lunch, we each grabbed something fast—a container of yogurt, a bag of chips, an apple—and ran out to the blacktop, where you could play basketball or run around, or just talk with your friends and breathe actual oxygen for thirty minutes.

Today was Omi's twelfth birthday, and we'd planned a surprise. While Max distracted her inside the cafeteria, Zara and I would run out to the blacktop and make a giant O out of pebbles. The O was my idea: her actual name was

Naomi-Jacinta Duarte Chavez, but we called her Omi for short.

And the thing about Omi was that she collected things from nature—seashells, bird feathers, stones in weird shapes and colors. So first we'd give Omi a birthday hug inside the O, and then we'd give her a little red pouch of chocolate pebbles—basically M&M's, but each one a different pebbly shape and color. It wouldn't be some generic babyish birthday celebration, with cupcakes for the whole class, like you did in elementary school. Just something personal and private, for our friends.

But what happened was, the exact second Zara and I stepped outside, Ms. Wardak, the lunch aide, blocked us. Usually she ignored us, and we ignored her back. Although not today, for some reason.

"Why are you girls out here?" she demanded. "You're supposed to go get lunch first."

"We know, but it's our friend's birthday," Zara said. "And we wanted to make her name out of pebbles."

"I'm sorry, *what*?" Ms. Wardak's whistle bounced on her chest.

"Just her first initial," I said.

"Out of *pebbles*?" Ms. Wardak asked. "That's a birthday present?"

Suddenly I was feeling a little sticky inside my fuzzy green sweater. We didn't have time for this conversation.

And we definitely didn't have time to explain seventh graders, if Ms. Wardak didn't understand things.

"It's not the *whole* present," I said quickly. "Just one little thing we wanted to do. And please, we really do need to hurry. Because our friend is coming out here any second, so."

Ms. Wardak sighed, like she didn't have the energy to argue that normal humans liked their presents pebble-free, and in boxes. "Fine. Just be sure you clean up the mess afterward, girls. I don't want any basketball players to trip."

"Oh, we won't be anywhere *near* the basketball hoop," Zara promised. "That's kind of the *opposite* of where we'll be. We're usually over where it's more private—"

I tugged her sleeve. Sometimes Zara didn't keep track of time very well. And anyway, I couldn't see a reason to share our lunchtime habits with Ms. Wardak.

We ran over to the far edge of the blacktop, where a strip of pebbles divided the ground into School and Not-School. Often during lunch my friends and I hung out here and just talked. Or sang (mostly that was Zara, who world-premiered her own compositions). Or pebble-hunted (mostly that was Omi, although sometimes me, too). One time Max and I joined a game called untag on the blacktop—not elementary school tag, but a whole different version, with crazy-complicated rules.

Although usually we hung out just the four of us, because I had band right after lunch, and we wouldn't be together the rest of the afternoon.

"Hey, Mila, look at this one—it's *literally purple!*" Zara shouted at me as she crouched over the pebbles. "And ooh, this one sort of looks like an arrowhead! Or Oklahoma!"

"We don't have time to pick individually." I scooped up a handful of pebbles and started laying them out on the blacktop. "Come on, Zara, just help make the O."

"All right, all right," she pretend-grumbled. "How big?"

"I don't know, big enough for the four of us to stand in, so it's like an O for Omi. And also a Circle of Friendship." I'd thought of that just now; although I couldn't decide if it was cute or stupid.

Zara loved it. "Circle of Friendship! Oooh, that's perfect, Mila!" She began singing. *"Cir-cle of Friennndshhhii—"*

"Eek, hurry! I see them coming!"

Max and Omi were scurrying toward us, dodging a basketball. I hadn't seen it happen, but somehow, over the past minute, a game had started on the other end of the blacktop. The usual boys—Callum, Leo, Dante, and Tobias—crashing into each other. Banging the ball against the blacktop: *thwump, thwump.* Shouting, laughing, cheering, arguing.

"Over *here!*" I could hear Callum shouting at the

others. His voice was always the one that reached my ears. "Here! Throw it to *me*!"

We finished the O just as our friends arrived.

"HAPPPYYY BIIIRRTHDAAAY!" Zara shouted, opening her arms wide. "Look, Omi, we made you an O! For your initial, and also a literal Circle of Friendship! Which was Mila's idea," she added, catching my eye.

Omi clapped her hands and laughed. "I love it, you guys—it's beautiful! Thank you! I'll treasure it always!"

"Well, maybe not *always*," I said, grinning. "It's just a temporary work of art."

"Yeah, you know, like a sand sculpture," Max said. His big blue eyes were shining. "Or have you ever seen a Buddhist sand mandala? They use these different colors of sand—it's incredibly cool—and then they destroy it. On purpose." Max's mom was a Buddhist, so he knew all sorts of things like that.

"Huh," Zara said. "Fascinating, Max, but a little off topic." She pulled Omi inside the O. "Birthday hug! Everyone in!"

The four of us crowded into the O and threw our arms around each other. Because I was shorter than everyone else, I found myself in the middle of the hug, staring straight into Zara's collarbone. I'd never noticed it before, but she had a tiny snail-shaped freckle on her neck, two shades darker than her light brown skin.

"Okay, this is great, but promise you *won't* sing 'Happy Birthday'!" Omi was giggling.

"Sorry, Omi, it's required by headquarters," Zara replied.

She began singing in her strong, clear alto. Still hugging, Max and I joined in, a bit off-key, but so what. We were just up to "Happy birthday, dear Oooo-mi" when something brushed my shoulders. A hand.

Suddenly we were surrounded by the basketball boys—Callum, Leo, Dante, and Tobias. They'd locked arms around us and were singing along. Well, sort of singing.

"Happy birthday to yooouuu," Callum shouted into my hair. His breath on my neck made me shiver.

Now the song was over, but the hug was still happening, Callum's hand clamping the fuzz of my green sweater. The basketball boys smelled like boy sweat and pizza. I told myself to breathe slowly, through my teeth.

"What are you doing, Leo?" Zara laughed, a bit too loudly. Or maybe it just felt loud because she was so close. "Who said you could join the hug?"

"Don't be nasty—we just wanted to say happy birthday," Leo said. "Not to *you*, Zara. To Omi."

Zara flinched. It was a quick-enough flinch that maybe I was the only one who noticed. But then, I knew all about Zara's giant crush on Leo, who had wavy, sandy-colored hair, greenish eyes, and just a few freckles. He was cute, but in a *Hey, don't you think I'm cute?* sort of way.

I wriggled my shoulder, but Callum's hand was squeezing. And not leaving.

Now I could feel my armpits getting damp.

"Well, thanks, but I'm kind of getting smooshed here," Omi called out. "So if you guys wouldn't mind—"

"Okay, sorry!" Leo said. "Happy birthday, Omi! Bye!"

All at once, like a flock of birds, they took off for the basketball court.

Immediately my friends and I pulled apart, and I could breathe normally again.

"Okay, that was weird," I said, brushing boy molecules off the fuzz of my sweater.

"Oh, Mila, don't be such a baby," Zara said. "They were just being friendly."

I snorted. "You think getting smooshed like that is *friendly*?"

"Yeah, Zara," Max said. "You're only saying that because you like Leo."

Zara gave a short laugh. "All right, Max, I agree, the whole thing was *incredibly awkward*, but I thought it was kind of sweet. Didn't you, Omi?"

"I don't know, I guess," Omi said. "Maybe." She shrugged, but she was smiling. Also blushing.

Max's long hair was in his face, so I couldn't see his eyes. "Well, they wrecked the O," he muttered.

He was right: the pebbles were scattered everywhere. No more Circle of Friendship, or O for Omi.

"Dang," I said. "Well, we did promise Ms. Wardak we'd clear off the pebbles. So we should put them back now anyway."

"Who's Ms. Wardak?" Omi asked.

"You know. The lunch aide." I started kicking the pebbles over to the edge of the asphalt, and so did Max.

"Oh, who cares about *her*, Mila," Zara said impatiently. "She's not even a teacher, and she doesn't pay attention." She grabbed Omi's hand. "We have another present for you, and it's so much better! Look!"

Zara reached into her jeans pocket and pulled out the little red sack of chocolate pebbles.

Omi screamed. "Omigod, you guys, I love these! How did you know?"

"Because we're your best friends and we *do* pay attention," Zara replied, beaming.

I almost added that they were my idea. But I decided that wouldn't be best-friendly.

SWISH

Aside from lunch, when I could be with my friends, my best time at school was definitely band. I could be having a boring or awful or just not very fun day, and then as soon as I started playing my trumpet, it felt like the skies were opening up. And I had this feeling of endless space, no people or clouds or even buildings anywhere. Just big wide fields of grass and a blank blue sky. Sometimes when I was playing, I even saw the color blue.

I don't mean I *literally saw* the color blue. I mean it *felt* like the color blue. Calm and open, like it could go on forever.

Also, it just felt good to get really loud. Because all day long, teachers were telling us to be quiet. *No talking, no laughing, no whispering.* Sometimes our math teacher even complained about "loud sighing." So band was the one time of the day when you could let it out. *Should* let it out, the louder the better.

And after that weirdness today at lunch, I *needed* band.

But as soon as I took my chair in the trumpet section, I could tell something was up. People were standing around, chatting, laughing nervously, instead of warming up their instruments.

"What's going on?" I asked the kid to my right, Rowan Crawley.

"Section leaders getting announced," he muttered. "And that means Callum, of course."

"Dude," Dante agreed. He shoved Callum playfully. Callum grinned.

I couldn't even look at him. Instead I took my trumpet out of its case, wiping it slowly and carefully with a little gray cloth. *Wipe, wipe, wipe.*

Ms. Fender tapped her music stand with her baton.

"Okay, people, here we go," she said. "I'm ready to announce this year's seventh grade band leaders."

Everyone stopped talking. Have you ever seen a tree full of chirping birds when a hawk or a fox appears? All of a sudden there isn't a peep. Just a sort of loud quiet. It was almost like that in the band room, except for chairs squeaking.

So it was weird that my heart was thumping. I mean,

I knew I played trumpet really well, and I'd even taken some private lessons over the summer with this cool high school girl named Emerson. But I didn't *really* think Ms. Fender would pick me for section leader. She was the kind of teacher who had special pets—people like Samira Spurlock on clarinet, and Annabel Cho on saxophone. Who I thought of as Pets Number One and Two.

And of the trumpet players, her favorite was Callum—Pet Number Three. We'd only been in seventh grade band for a couple of weeks, but already she'd made that clear. As soon as she handed out a new piece of music, she'd ask him to stand up and play it, not just for the trumpet section, but for the whole band. I'm not saying he wasn't a good player—and it wasn't that I was jealous. But I couldn't help wondering: Why was it always *him*?

"First I want to make clear that being chosen section leader is an honor, but also a big responsibility," Ms. Fender was saying. "So if you don't practice your instrument every day, you will quickly lose your position." She gave the whole band a stern look over her music stand. "We have a very ambitious program this year, and I'm going to need leaders I can count on. We *all* do."

Ms. Fender paused as she flipped her honey-colored hair over one shoulder. Music teachers know about timing.

And now she was smiling. "All right, then, without further ado: here are our seventh grade band leaders.

Please stand when I call your name. For clarinets, Samira Spurlock. For saxophones, Annabel Cho. For trumpets, Callum Burley—"

Hey, what a surprise. Pets Number One, Two, and Three.

Dante, who played trumpet, and Leo, who played sax, started cheering like they were at a basketball game. Tobias (trombone) actually whistled.

Callum stood, raking his floppy brown hair out of his dark brown eyes, blushing and smiling at his friends. And when he bowed—a sort of bow in quotation marks, as if he were wearing a tuxedo—his hand swished across my shoulder.

Had he noticed this? It was hard to imagine that he hadn't—my sweater was green and fuzzy, so unless his hand was expecting to collide with a Muppet or something, he should have been startled. Although he'd already touched my sweater during Omi's birthday hug, and actually, this hand swish was much quicker, more random, than the shoulder squeeze.

Still, it was the kind of contact that meant you should apologize. Even if he hadn't hurt my shoulder.

But when I looked at him, he didn't say anything or even glance in my direction. Probably he was focused on Ms. Fender, looking cool to his friends, making an impression on the entire band.

Who were all smiling at him, clapping. So of course that's what I did too.

DINETTE

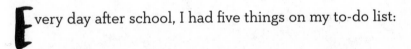

Every day after school, I had five things on my to-do list:

1) Walk Delilah (sweet, scruffy, stinky rescue
   mutt, age ten).
2) Wait at bus stop for Hadley (bratty little
   sister, age six).
3) Do homework.
4) Practice trumpet.
5) Make dinner.

Well, that's sort of an exaggeration. I didn't "make" dinner; I heated it. Mom worked full-time—Dad had left years ago—so it was my job to turn on the oven and pop in one of the dishes she'd precooked and stuck in the freezer for the school week. Mom was always exhausted when she got home from office-managing ("totally wiped out" was her expression), but she always wanted to hear all the details about school while the three of us sat together around the little dinette table for dinner.

And she especially wanted to hear about friend stuff. Sometimes it felt like she was listening for something specific, although I could never tell what that was.

"So did Omi like her candy?" Mom asked that evening, as we finished up a pot of veggie chili.

"What candy?" Hadley demanded.

"For her birthday," I said. "Yeah, she loved it—"

"Was it a Milky Way?"

"What?"

"Was it that dark chocolate kind? I *hate* that kind. But white chocolate is worse. It tastes like soap."

"No, Hadley, it wasn't a Milky Way. It was these chocolate pebbles—"

"Chocolate *what*?"

I sighed. "Just chocolate shaped like little pebbles, okay?"

"Why did you give her *that*?" Hadley scrunched up her face.

"Because Omi collects pebbles, and other stuff. Max's mom got them at a fancy candy store. Never mind." Seriously, Hadley was harder to talk to than Ms. Wardak. "Anyway, we gave them to her outside, during lunch. But then these stupid boys came over and ruined everything—"

"Boys?" Mom asked, wiping her mouth with her napkin.

"Just some basketball players. You don't know them. In our grade." Already I had the feeling that I'd said too much. Which was weird, because I hadn't said anything, really. "Anyway, Omi loved the chocolate pebbles," I added quickly.

"Mila, you know what I want for my birthday?" Hadley said. "*Not* pebbles."

"Sure," I said, smiling. "We'll definitely get you not-pebbles. We'll get you rocks and gravel and boulders—"

"*I don't want any gravel or boulders!*"

"Sure you do. Giant ones made of white chocolate—"

Hadley squealed and slapped my arm. It didn't hurt, but I yelled "Ow" anyway.

"Mila, no teasing," Mom scolded. Her voice was sharper than I expected. Even Hadley looked surprised.

"Okay, fine," I said. "But tell Hadley not to slap!"

"No slapping," Mom agreed. "Hadley, tell Mila you're sorry."

"Sorry," Hadley said. She crossed her arms and stuck out her tongue at me. "But I don't want Mila to give me any *white chocolate*. Or boulders."

"I'll try my best to remember that." I almost stuck out my tongue back at her. But I didn't, because that would be babyish.

SWEATER

It's funny how close friends can be totally different about certain things. Like when it came to clothes: Zara wore neon-colored tees with funny sayings, even in the most freezing weather. Max just always wore a faded navy hoodie with a droopy pocket in the front and baggy gray sweatpants. Of all of us, Omi was the one who paid the most attention to what she looked like; I knew (because she told me) that before school every morning, she spent a full hour choosing her outfit, doing her long dark hair. Omi wasn't vain or stuck-up or anything like that, but she really cared how she looked. I mean, cared a *lot*.

As for me, I was somewhere in the middle. I didn't just throw on a tee like Zara, but I didn't fuss over my appearance either. My hair was easy, just a thick, medium-brown, medium-length ponytail—although, to be honest, lately I'd been more focused on my clothes. Because even though I was still pretty short, over the summer I'd had a sort of growth spurt or something, and now my jeans were getting snug around my hips. Also my tops were getting tight across my chest, digging into my armpits. But I didn't want to ask Mom to take me shopping; the way she kept asking Hadley and me if we "really needed" our favorite breakfast cereals, or if we could "stretch our shampoo" for another week, I could tell money was kind of a problem for us these days.

So lately what I did was just keep wearing the fuzzy green sweater. Not only did it fit across my chest, but also it was long enough to cover the top of my jeans. Wearing the sweater, I didn't wonder how I looked, because I knew: basically like a fuzzy green potato.

Also, the fuzz was comforting, like going to school covered in old teddy bear. Even if sometimes it felt a little too warm.

Of course Hadley gave me a hard time about it at breakfast. "Mila, why are you wearing that sweater *again*?"

"Because I like it," I said as I poured some cardboard-tasting store-brand cereal into my bowl. All the kinds we had came in giant boxes with names that sounded like real cereals' weird second cousins—Oaties. Krisp-o's. Hunny Flakes. Korn Klusters. The trick was eating them fast, before you actually tasted them, and before they turned all slushy from milk.

Hadley didn't even bother with milk. She ate her Oaties dry and cardboard-tasting, straight from the box. "But probally it's really, really smelly by now. You want me to sniff it for you?"

She made a dog-sniff face.

"No *thank* you," I said.

Mom looked up from her coffee. "Mila, seriously, though. I'm sure that sweater could use some washing. You've already worn it twice this week—"

"She wore it last week too," Hadley pointed out.

"Thanks for keeping score." I glared at her. "It's fine, Mom. Anyhow, I'm using deodorant."

"De-*odor*-ant," Hadley repeated, giggling so hard she went sideways off her chair.

"Hadley, stop fooling and drink some milk," Mom said. "Mila, no one's saying that sweater smells."

"*Smells*," Hadley repeated, still giggling.

Mom ignored her. "But it can't possibly be clean after all that wearing. And at your age, honey, you need to pay attention to hygiene. It's important."

I groaned loudly. "Fine, I'll wash my sweater after school. Is everyone happy now?"

"Mila." Mom sighed.

Work was stressful enough, I knew. She didn't need an argument from me at breakfast.

"Sorry," I said, suddenly feeling ashamed of myself.

Mom got up from the table and kissed my cheek. "It's okay. Maybe this weekend we can take a shopping trip to Old Navy."

"Really?"

"Me too." Hadley crunched a mouthful of Oaties. "I want new pj's with monkeys on them and snow boots and a pink down vest."

"We'll see," Mom replied. "Don't forget, baby, we're on a budget."

"*Budget*," Hadley repeated. "That's a good name for a hamster."

I rolled my eyes. My little sister had a way of zooming off topic. "Hadley, we're not getting a hamster. We already have a dog—"

"*If* we get a hamster."

"Well, *if* we get a hamster, which we're *not*, we're definitely not naming it Budget!"

"Girls," Mom said distractedly. She checked her watch. "Yikes, I'm already late. And that Robert Reinhold—"

I looked up. "You mean your new boss? What about him?"

"Oh, he's just been giving me a hard time. Never mind."

Mom stepped into her black work pumps. "Come on, baby, let's get you to the bus stop. Mila, if you want me to drive you this morning, you'd better be ready the second I get back. And seriously, sweetheart, when you get home from school today—"

"I'll wash my sweater, Mom, I promise."

Mom blew me a kiss as she led Hadley out the door.

HUG

esterday, after Ms. Fender had announced the section leaders, she'd assigned the rest of us our chairs based on how good she thought we were as musicians. I was second chair in the trumpet section. Second best, which meant I was seated right next to Callum.

"Although chairs may change over the course of the year," Ms. Fender had told us, "depending on your commitment to rehearsing, and your focus during class." *Also on whether I decree that you're my pet,* I mentally added as I inched my music stand away from Callum's.

Ms. Fender had also handed out some new music—"Pirate Medley"—which we were supposed to start practicing at home. Stupidly, I'd forgotten to pack my music folder in my backpack this morning, which meant that today I'd be coming to band unprepared, already endangering my position as second chair. So when I got to school, I went straight to the band room, hoping to find an extra copy of the sheet music.

The band room was empty when I got there. But a second later Callum, Leo, and Dante stepped inside, laughing in a rowdy way that for some reason made my stomach knot. What were they all doing in here, anyway?

They stopped for a basketball-teamish huddle over by the door.

I pretended not to notice.

"Hey, Mila," Leo called out from across the room.

"Oh, hi," I said as I scanned the shelves for "Pirate Medley." "Do you know where Ms. Fender keeps extra sheet music?"

"What for?" Dante asked.

"I forgot to bring my music folder. And I wanted to look at 'Pirate Medley' before band today." Why was I explaining this to them? It wasn't their business.

"I'll let you borrow mine if you give Leo a birthday hug," Dante said.

What?

I glanced at Dante, then at Leo. Maybe I hadn't heard that right.

"Excuse me?" I said.

"Yeah, Mila, today's my birthday." Leo smiled. A cute-boy sort of smile.

"It is?" I said.

"Why, you think I'd lie about my birthday?"

Callum was nodding. Not looking at me, though. "Yeah, it's definitely his birthday. He's having a bowling party this weekend. With pizza and chocolate cake."

"And one of those papier-mâché donkeys," Dante added.

"You mean a piñata," Leo said. "And that's just for little kids, moron. Anyway, Mila, if you don't want to give me a birthday hug, it's cool. My feelings aren't hurt *at all*."

Dante laughed and slapped Leo on the shoulder. Callum kept smiling.

I could feel the back of my neck getting damp and my heart speeding.

What exactly was going on here? Whatever it was, it felt weird.

And where was Ms. Fender? For someone with perfect timing, she should be walking in here right now.

Right now.

Right . . . now.

"Whoa, Mila, don't you think that's a little nasty?" Dante was saying. "We all hugged Omi for *her* birthday, didn't we?"

Nobody asked you to. Plus, you messed up the O.

"Zara hugged Leo five minutes ago," Callum added. "On the bus."

She did? Well, because she likes him, that's why.

Now I could hear Zara scolding me. *Oh, Mila, why are you being such a baby? They're just being friendly. Yes, incredibly awkwardly, but—*

And then I had this thought: *They haven't moved from the door. I'll need to pass them to get out of here.*

This isn't a choice.

"Okay, fine," I said, pretending to laugh. I walked over to Leo, threw my arms around him and squeezed once. "Happy birthday."

"Fuzzy sweater," he replied, grinning.

MOTHS

*Z*ara was a head taller than most of our classmates, with black hair piled on top of her head in a big puff. So even though our homerooms were at opposite ends of the hallway, I spotted her right away, just as she was about to walk inside.

Should I wait until we were together at lunch? *Maybe I should*, I told myself.

Except my stomach was doing this fluttery-moth sort of thing. Which wasn't the same as a fluttery-butterfly thing. Because butterflies were soft and pretty, but moths just gave me the creeps.

I ran down the hallway, calling her name. She didn't hear me right away, or maybe she wasn't fully awake. Zara had plenty of energy once she got going, but we all knew she wasn't a morning person.

When I caught up to her, I pulled her over to the wall outside her homeroom. Today she was wearing a red tee that said NO SMORKING. A lot of her tees were bad translations into English; her dad thought they were hilarious, so he was always buying her new ones.

"What's up?" she asked in a foggy voice.

"Nothing," I said quickly. "Can I ask you a question?"

"Obviously." She yawned without covering her mouth.

"Well, this is sort of weird, but . . ." I paused. "Did you hug Leo on the bus just before? Like we did for Omi yesterday?"

"Leo?" Zara blinked. She was finally waking up. "Why would I do that?"

"You know. For his birthday."

"You mean today?"

I nodded.

"Mila, Leo's birthday is in December."

"It is?" More moth flutters. "How do you know that?"

"Because I just do." Like: *Of course I'd know my crush's birthday.* Her brow wrinkled. "Why are you asking?"

"I don't know," I said. "I think I misheard something before. It's not important."

The bell rang for homeroom.

We looked at each other.

The moths fluttered.

Should I tell Zara about the band room? How Leo and his friends had lied about her? And basically tricked me into hugging Leo?

I desperately needed to share this information with my friend.

But something in her eyes—it felt sharp and stinging, like a slap—made me stop.

"Never mind," I said brightly. "See you at lunch, Zara, okay?"

"Yeah, okay," Zara said, shrugging.

TRUTH

The way seventh grade worked, you were on an academic "team" with kids who took the same language. I took Spanish, Zara and Omi took French, and Max took Latin. Also, I was the only one of us in band. And what this meant was that we were together—the four of us—exactly one period a day, which was lunch.

So that whole morning, while I basically sleepwalked though science, math, ELA, and Spanish, I couldn't stop replaying the scene in the band room. The whole thing had felt strange and creepy, so why hadn't I just walked out of the room? Or even thought of a lame comeback (*No hug, but I'll play you "Happy Birthday" on my trumpet*)? Why hadn't I challenged Leo's birthday in the first place?

The more I thought about it, the more obvious it was the boys had been lying.

And why hadn't I told Zara the truth? A big part of me was furious for not talking. When something happens, and it's weird or embarrassing, you're supposed to tell your best friends, aren't you? Or at least feel like you *can* tell them. So why had I made myself shut up in the hallway with Zara? Because it wasn't as if *I'd* done anything I should be ashamed about, if you didn't count stupidly agreeing to a hug, which really, I'd needed to do to escape the band room.

What I just kept telling myself was that I was trying to protect Zara's feelings. Because the two of us were such close friends; so obviously, I knew how much she liked Leo, how she worried he didn't like her back. I also knew that underneath the loud, jokey, songwriting Zara was the super-sensitive Zara, who cried at Disney movies and had this crazy idea that she was ugly (too tall, too skinny, too something). And if I'd told her that after hugging Omi yesterday, Leo (for some mysterious reason) had wanted to hug *me*, she'd definitely feel terrible about that. So it was really the truth—or at least part of the truth—that I'd stopped talking because I didn't want to hurt her.

Also, there was this other thing about Zara: if her feelings were hurt, she could be nasty. Afterward she always apologized, but she couldn't unsay what she'd just said.

Like, one time this past summer when we were at the town pool together, she refused to come out of the bathroom, because Leo was swimming in the deep section, and she didn't want him to see her in a bathing suit.

"He'll think I'm a toothpick, Mila," she said. She laughed, but in a scared sort of way.

"Aw, come on, who cares what he thinks," I said.

"*I* do." Her face crumpled. "And Mila, can you please *try* not to be so immature. Or maybe just fake it, like you usually do, okay?"

Which was totally unfair, and we both knew it.

Of course, right away she told me she was sorry, and I forgave her. But still.

Zara was a fun, caring friend, but she was capable of meanness. And after the hug business in the band room, maybe I just didn't want to risk another weird conversation.

LUCK

The whole morning, I watched the basketball boys out of the corner of my eye. It was strange how none of them looked at me, like maybe the hug hadn't even happened. The other possibility was that the hug *had* happened, but it was just a meaningless blip in their day, and they'd already forgotten about it. After all, I told myself, these boys had pretty much ignored me before this morning, so maybe they'd just ignore me again from now on.

Except one time, in the hallway right before third period, I thought Dante might have bumped into me on purpose. Maybe. The halls were crowded, and there was always jostling and shoving by the staircase, so I wasn't positive he could have avoided it.

But when I looked at him, I saw a little half-smile

creeping across his face. Although possibly he was just thinking about a private joke.

I mean, I wasn't *sure* he was smiling about bumping into me. I wasn't even totally sure he was *smiling*. Or that he realized he'd bumped into *me*.

But afterward I had small random motions in my stomach, almost like hiccups.

Finally, the bell rang for lunch, and I found Omi in the cafeteria line to get yogurt. She lived with her grandparents, who always made a giant fuss about birthdays and holidays, and as the two of us walked onto the blacktop, Omi was describing the birthday feast her abuela had made her yesterday, all the presents she'd gotten, how her cake had the kind of candles with sparklers.

"You're so lucky, Omi," I told her.

She smiled. "I know, right? And they're already planning my quinceañera."

"They *are*? But that's three years from now!"

"Well, my abuela is very organized. She's already picked out her dress."

I tried, but I couldn't imagine this. Our house seemed like such chaos compared to Omi's, like we went from day to day, meal to meal, with barely any plans at all. I knew Mom was working crazy hard all the time, and even so, we could only afford the cheap cereal. So it's not that I blamed her for any of it.

But I couldn't help wondering what it would be like to live in Omi's house, with two grown-ups paying attention to every little thing you wanted or did. Planning parties for you years ahead of time.

Would that be better? Or hard, but in a different way?

"Ooh, Mila, I almost forgot, look at this!" Omi reached into her pocket, opened her hand, and showed me a tiny red feather. "It's from a scarlet tanager. Tía Rosario found it in the Dominican Republic and just brought it back for me. Isn't it beautiful?"

"Yeah," I said, wondering what it was like having aunts who brought you bird feathers. Also being the sort of person who collected them.

Suddenly Tobias ran over to us.

"Hey," he said, so loudly it made me flinch. "Hi, Omi. Hi, Mila."

"Hi," Omi said in the floaty voice she was using lately when she spoke to boys. She slipped the feather back into her pocket.

I snuck a look at Tobias. He was smaller than the other basketball boys, skinnier, with dark fuzz on his upper lip and a few pink zits on his forehead. Tobias played trombone in band, but he was the only basketball boy who hadn't been in the band room this morning. So I wasn't sure how to respond. If I should respond at all.

And now he was smiling. Not at Omi. At me.

"So, Mila, can I get a hug?" he asked.

"Excuse me?" I said coldly, pretending not to notice Omi's surprise.

"You know, like you gave Leo." His mouth was still smiling, but his eyes were darting around, as if he wanted to know who was watching. And his voice wobbled a little. Was he nervous about something?

Omi looked confused. "Mila, wait. You hugged Leo . . . ?"

"Because he told me it was his birthday." I could feel my armpits start to drip. "Which was a lie. And he asked for a birthday hug, which I'm pretty mad about, actually. So I don't understand why *you* want a hug, Tobias. Unless it's *your* fake birthday too."

"Nah," he said. A blush was creeping up his neck. "It's just for luck."

"Luck?" Omi repeated.

"Yeah, for our game. Yesterday when we all hugged you"—Tobias nodded at Omi—"the guys who touched Mila's sweater scored a personal best. So we decided that Mila's green fuzz was magic. Or something."

I burst out laughing.

Seriously? This was the reason for the hug? Their stupid *basketball game*?

No, it was beyond stupid. But also, in a way I couldn't explain, a huge relief.

34

"Tobias, my sweater can't possibly make anyone score baskets," I said.

"No, no, Mila, I really think it does," Tobias said. But the way he said this, it seemed like more of a question. Like he was trying to convince himself. "What's it made out of, anyway?"

"I think it's mohair," Omi said.

"*Mole* hair?" Tobias asked.

"No, *mo*. Whatever that is." She laughed.

Of course I knew it wasn't mohair. It was something synthetic that you could throw in the washing machine. But that probably meant it was cheap, so I didn't say it.

"Well, whatever your sweater is, Mila, can I please have a hug?" Tobias asked quickly.

By now he seemed like he'd changed his mind and just wanted to get away. I could see him glancing at the boys gathering under the basketball hoop, waiting for him to start their game. And then Leo made a *hurry up* arm motion at Tobias: *Come on, we're waiting.*

"No, Tobias, you can't," I said. "Sorry."

He winced.

I couldn't help it; I felt sorry for him.

Without thinking, I held out my left arm. "But I guess it's okay if you touch the sleeve," I added.

"Awesome," Tobias said. He rubbed my elbow like it was a genie lamp.

But then, before I knew it was happening, he threw his arms around my chest and squeezed so hard that for a second I lost my breath.

Under the basketball hoop, the boys cheered.

A moth fluttered inside my stomach. Two moths.

"Thanks," Tobias muttered. He ran off to join the basketball boys, who slapped his back and said things I couldn't hear.

Now Zara and Max had joined us. Although Max was hanging back behind Zara, like maybe he might want to make an escape.

"What was *that* about?" Zara asked. She made the sort of face you do when something smells bad.

Omi shrugged. "The boys think Mila's sweater is good luck."

"For basketball," I added quickly. "It's stupid."

Zara snorted. "Why would they think *that*?"

I tried to look at Max, but he'd turned away, watching something or someone across the blacktop.

"Who knows," I said. "They have this dumb superstition."

"Or maybe Tobias just likes you, Mila," Omi said in a teasing voice.

"No, Callum likes Mila," Zara declared.

"Me?" Where had she gotten *that* from? I made a noise like *pffft*. "Zara, I'm positive he doesn't, okay? Callum's a total jerk to me in band. But even if he did, what does that have to do with Tobias?"

"Maybe they *both* like you," Omi said. She was grinning now.

"Okay, that's crazy," I said. "Anyhow, I *told* Tobias he couldn't hug me, but he did it anyway."

Zara kicked some pebbles. "Well, Mila, no one can hug you if you don't let them," she said, not smiling, not looking at me.

BUS

Most mornings Mom drove me to school on her way to work, and I took the school bus home. I wasn't crazy about the bus—it was loud; sometimes there were fights; often there was teasing—but it was the fastest way I could get home to my dog Delilah, who desperately needed to pee.

And that afternoon when I got on Bus 6 West, I felt nothing but relief. It had been a long, strange day—the hug in the band room, the explanation from Tobias, but then the way he hugged me after I'd said no. Plus Zara, who'd acted so funny with me at lunch. The more I thought about it, the less I could explain exactly what was weird about her behavior—just like usual, she'd complained about her mom, sung a song she was writing (called "Cheater"), and insisted she'd never get a solo in chorus (despite us swearing she had a great voice). But still, every time Zara's eyes met mine, I almost felt something chilly pass over me, like how seeing a ghost is supposed to give you goose bumps.

So it was a relief to finally get on the bus. And because I was the first one, I took my favorite seat for zoning out: last row, left window.

Today this was a mistake.

"Hey, thanks, Mila, you saved us a seat!" Leo yelled out as he and the basketball boys made it down the bus aisle.

My heart was thumping as I stared out the window, pretending not to hear.

"I'm sitting next to Mila, okay?" Dante said. Although it wasn't clear who he was asking. He sat down heavily, not taking off his backpack, which jabbed into my side. "You're okay with this, Mila, right?"

"Why wouldn't she be?" Leo said. "She likes us." He took the seat in front of me, turned around, and grinned. "You do like us, Mila, don't you?"

Three rows in front, Annabel Cho and Samira Spurlock were watching. So was Hunter Schultz, who'd teased Max last year until Max told the assistant principal.

"I really don't care *what* you do," I muttered. "Any of you."

"See? She's okay with it. I told you," Leo said to Tobias, who was smiling, even though his neck was turning red.

Callum took the seat directly across the aisle. His floppy brown hair covered his eyes, and he didn't say anything.

Annabel whispered something to Samira, who nodded. The bus started.

As soon we pulled out of the parking lot and turned the corner down Main Street, I could feel Dante's shoulder bump against mine. He was wearing track shorts; his legs were spread in front of him in a forty-five-degree angle, so he was taking two-thirds of the seat.

This definitely felt wrong and unfair. I mean, all I even knew about Dante Paul was that his family was from Haiti and he was supposed to be some sort of computer genius. And now his bare legs kept brushing against my jeans.

I pretended not to notice for the first block. And the second. And the third.

But when the bus hit a giant pothole, his arm flew across my chest.

"Hey, Dante, watch your arm," I said. "And please move over, okay?"

Dante looked surprised. Maybe too surprised. "You want me to move over?"

"Yeah. We're supposed to be sharing this seat equally, aren't we? And I'm getting squished."

"Oh. Sorry," he said.

Right away I thought: *Okay, Mila, now you're being*

paranoid. The seat isn't wide enough; he can't help it if he smooshes into you. And that pothole wasn't his fault.

Except the thing was, he didn't budge. His legs stayed spread and his shoulder kept bumping.

Bump. Bump. Bump.

Every bump seemed to burn my shoulder.

And just as we were pulling up to my bus stop, I turned to him. "Excuse me, Dante," I said. My voice was squeaking. "I'm getting off now. So you need to stand up, okay?"

"What?"

I raised my voice, but it didn't just get louder. It got squeakier. "I mean to let me pass. We're at my stop now—?"

Leo turned around. "That's okay. Mila, you can get past him. Just squeeze."

Tobias and Dante snickered. Callum didn't say anything. Hunter, Annabel, and Samira stared at me.

I froze; I couldn't get out of the seat.

"Fielding Street," the bus driver called out. "Let's move it, guys."

Now my face was on fire. I stood to push past Dante, who threw his legs in my way as if he were blocking me from scoring a basket.

And just as I made it to the aisle, I heard Callum's voice behind me.

"Hey, Mila, wear your fuzzy sweater tomorrow," he called out as the other boys collapsed in laughter.

MIRROR

Normally I had to pick up Hadley at her bus stop, but today she had a playdate at her friend Tyler's. So this meant that when I got home, I had the house all to myself, which felt like the first good thing about the entire day.

As soon as I'd had a glass of water and a handful of Korn Krunch (this sweet and sticky store-brand kind of snack Mom always bought), I went into the bathroom and stared at the mirror.

What are the boys seeing?

My sweater went all the way up to my collarbone, and all the way down to my hips. Nothing was showing, or poking out.

And yes, I had boobs and a butt, just like plenty of girls

in seventh grade—but no one had ever made any comments about them. At least, to my face.

I wasn't fat, or skinny like Zara. Ugly, or pretty like Omi. As far as I could tell, I was just average-looking, really. Right smack in the middle when it came to seventh grade girls.

>*Are people—*
>*and by people, I mean the basketball boys—*
>*seeing something about me that I can't?*
>*Am I missing something about myself?*
>*Something obvious?*

PRACTICE

At supper Hadley told us about a kid in her class who ate a grasshopper.

"But probally he didn't *swallow* it," she added.

"That doesn't make it any better," I informed her. "If he chewed it in his mouth—"

"Girls," Mom said. "Not table talk." She frowned at a text sound on her phone, then got up from the table and went into her bedroom.

"Well, but if he didn't swallow it, it's not in his *stomach*," Hadley argued.

"Uh-huh," I said, giving up.

I sat there for ten more minutes, but Mom didn't come back, so Hadley and I cleared the table. Then I rinsed all the dishes and put them in the dishwasher. Maybe Mom had gotten a text from Dad: he'd moved out a little while after Hadley was born, but I knew they still fought about money. "Child support," I'd overheard Mom saying through her closed bedroom door. Shouting it, sometimes.

And I'd always think: *How could someone forget to support a child?*

Even someone like Dad, who hadn't been around much when he lived here. And when he *was* around, was always yelling.

But at Mom, though. Never at me.

Although the thing about Dad was, he could hurt your feelings without yelling too. One time, when I was about five, I remember begging him to carry me on his back, and he said, "No, Mila, you're getting too heavy. If you want me to play with you, keep away from the cookies!" Mom scolded him for saying that, and he just laughed. Which was the worst part, if you really thought about it.

And in first grade I wore a cherry jelly bean costume for Halloween, and Dad said, "Well, I guess Mila's pretty princess days are over." When I burst into tears, Mom hugged me and said, "Dad is just noticing you don't wear princess costumes anymore, not that you aren't pretty!" And Dad didn't say, *Oh, Mila, of course that's what I meant!* He didn't say anything, actually.

There were plenty of other times I could remember when Dad said mean things, or things that were just mean enough. Or said nothing when he should have said something. Until finally he just packed up and left, and except for one birthday present when I was six, I didn't hear another word from him, ever.

So the truth was, even if I wanted to feel bad about him, even if I tried to miss him, I couldn't.

I went to my own room and shut the door.

My room was tiny—just enough space for a bed, a dresser, and a desk—but with its pale green curtains and the daisy-chain quilt Mom had found last summer at a yard sale, it was bright and cozy. Although maybe the best thing about it was that it was mine: an escape from Hadley, a place to practice my trumpet in private.

Which was what I'd been planning all supper. Now I opened the music case, took out my trumpet, and wiped the mouthpiece with the little gray cloth. Just like Emerson had taught me over the summer, first I warmed up with a few long notes.

Then I took my music folder off my desk, where I'd left it last night. "Pirate Medley" was right on top, waiting for me.

I took a deep breath.

No music I'd played all last year, including over the summer with Emerson, had given me any trouble. But this piece had tricky fingering, and weird notes you had to hold until you were dizzy. Also, there were barely any rests, so once it started, you were playing until your lips were numb and your lungs collapsed.

And the thing was, I knew that with Callum right next to me, I could actually just fake-play, the way some kids did. He was so loud that you could barely hear the other trumpets anyway.

But this idea—letting Callum play *for* me, basically—made my skin prickle. Because I cared about trumpet. Maybe I wasn't the best (according to Ms. Fender), but I was definitely good.

And if this stupid "Pirate Medley" was hard, then I just needed to practice, I told myself.

> *Over and over.*
> *Until my fingers know exactly what to do,*
> *and everything in my room disappears.*
> *Everything in my head, too.*
> *And all I see*
> *is the big open blue sky.*

PLAID

The next morning I came to breakfast in my pajamas.

"Mila, why aren't you dressed yet?" Mom scolded me. "I need to get to work early if I'm going to make my exercise class tonight."

"You're taking an exercise class?" I asked. "Since when?"

"Actually, it's Pilates, at that new place in town. They're offering free classes to get people to join. But my boss said I needed to be at my desk by eight this morning if I plan to leave work by four forty-five." She nibbled her bagel. "And don't change the subject, please. Why are you still in pajamas?"

Hadley crunched her dry Oaties. "I think Mila forgot to wash her sweater, that's why," she said in a tattletale sort of voice.

I glared at my little sister. "For your information, I didn't forget, okay?"

Which was the truth. Last night, after I finished practicing trumpet, I put my sweater in the washing machine. All by itself, so that it wouldn't shed green fuzz all over everything.

When it was done washing, I put it in the dryer for forty minutes.

And when it was dry, I stuffed it in the corner of my closet, underneath some old jeans I'd stopped wearing two years ago.

"I just got tired of wearing it," I said. "And nothing else fits me anymore. Mom, you said we'd go shopping this weekend—"

Mom sipped her coffee. "Well, that's the plan, sweetheart. I hope we can. I may need to go into work for a bit."

Really? But she never worked on weekends.

"What for?" I asked.

"Extra stuff. Maybe just an hour or two. Don't worry about it."

"I'm not worried. I just want to go to Old Navy. Like you *promised*."

Mom's frown made me realize that I'd sounded fresher than I'd meant. Oops. "So anyway," I added quickly, "until we *do* go shopping, can I please borrow something?"

"You mean from me?" Mom asked.

I nodded.

Mom put down her coffee.

"Seriously, Mila, why do you want to wear my clothes? They aren't right for school."

"Well, yeah, the worky stuff isn't," I agreed. "But what about that red plaid shirt—"

"You mean the one I wore to paint the bathroom?"

I nodded.

"First of all, it still has paint spatters."

"I don't mind."

"And second of all—"

"It looks like a tablecloth." Hadley started giggling. "Or a blanket for Delilah's dog bed."

Mom smiled. "It does not. It's just a comfortable old flannel shirt. But really, Mila, I'm *sure* it's too big!"

"Well, I think it's fine," I argued. "Anyway, I'll wear it over something. So it's *supposed* to be big."

"I guess that could look okay," Mom said. I could see her mom-wheels turning. "But why do you want to? Are your friends criticizing your wardrobe?"

I shook my head.

"Is it Omi? Sweetheart, I know her grandparents like to buy her nice things—"

"Omi is the prettiest," Hadley announced.

"It's not about Omi," I said quickly. "I just hate all my clothes, nothing fits, and I really, *really* want to wear that shirt. I think it'll look cool. *Please?*"

Mom glanced at her watch. "All right, fine, Mila. But I'm serious—we absolutely need to leave in two minutes, or I'll really hear it from Robert."

"Robert *who*?" Hadley asked.

"My new boss, baby. Robert Reinhold."

"His name sounds like *rrrrrr*. Like a growl," Hadley said. She made a growling-dog face.

"It certainly does, Had." Mom sighed. "So Mila, just get dressed really fast, okay? And grab a granola bar for breakfast. You can eat it in the car—"

"Hey, how come Mila gets to eat a granola bar for breakfast? In the *car*?" Hadley protested.

Because I'll be wearing a tablecloth.

EARLY

I got to school twenty-five minutes early that morning. When Ms. Wardak saw me in the hallway outside my locked homeroom, she asked if there wasn't "somewhere else" I could be.

"Actually, I'm okay right here," I told her.

"Young lady," Ms. Wardak snapped. "Don't give me attitude, or I'll report you to Mr. McCabe. Is that what you want?"

I shook my head. Mr. McCabe, the assistant principal, had a fleshy pink face and a look in his eyes that said *Don't mess with me.* I knew he wasn't evil or anything; after all, he'd stopped Hunter from bothering Max last year. But he was still in charge of punishments, so I definitely didn't want to get reported.

And honestly, I hadn't *meant* to give Ms. Wardak any attitude. Maybe there was something in my voice I didn't know about. This wouldn't be surprising—it was as if lately I'd been losing track of myself. What I looked like. What I sounded like.

"Sorry," I mumbled. "I just meant I felt okay. Here. Waiting for homeroom."

"Well, homeroom isn't happening anytime soon, so find a place *to be*," she said. "A hallway is not a place."

I almost asked what it was, then, if it wasn't a place—but there was a good chance Ms. Wardak would think that was more attitude.

So first I went to the first floor girls' room, but then a janitor came in to disinfect, and I had to leave. I knew the lunchroom wasn't a possibility; Hunter Schultz and some of his friends hung out there in the mornings, playing Magic cards until homeroom. And after Max's problems last year, I knew to keep away from Hunter myself.

When I spotted Ms. Wardak circling back to my hallway, I made a quick decision: I'd go to the band room, but only if Ms. Fender was there.

No way would I go in there alone, even if I wasn't wearing The Sweater.

BAND

"ood morning, Mila!" Ms. Fender greeted me. Today she
had on a blue dress with yellow roses, and her honey-
colored hair was loose around her shoulders. Sometimes I
tried to guess how old she was, but it was hard to tell. For
all I knew, she had kids.

Which was funny to think about, actually, considering
the way she had favorite students. Maybe as a mom she
had favorite babies. *You can have this rattle, but you just
have to watch....*

"Hi," I said. "I'm early today, so. Okay if I practice until
homeroom?"

She took a sip out of her fancy water bottle. It was
white, with gray swirls on it to make it look like marble,
and it had a twist-off lid made of metal. I wondered if Ms.

Fender had bought it for herself; it was hard to imagine being the kind of person who spent money on fake-marble water bottles.

"Of course, Mila," she said nicely. "You're always welcome here to work on your music. How are you finding 'Pirate Medley'?"

"It's okay. Although the middle section is a little hard."

"Well, watch your section leader. Callum has the fingering perfectly. I can ask him to show you—"

"No, that's okay," I cut in.

Ms. Fender raised her perfectly shaped eyebrows. You were supposed to follow the leader, who in my case was Pet Number Three. For a second I thought she'd remind me about that, but she pressed her lips together instead.

The door opened, and Pet Number One walked in. Samira Spurlock said hello to Ms. Fender, then went over to her chair. She opened her backpack, took out a sheet of music, and brought it over to Ms. Fender.

"My little brother spilled glue all over the table last night," Samira said. "So now all my papers are sticky. Can I please have a new 'Pirate Medley'?"

"Of course," Ms. Fender said. "I grew up with a little brother too, so I know how it goes." She winked at Samira. Actually *winked*. "Let me make you another copy, dear. One second."

She took Samira's music and left the room.

Samira glanced at me through her blue glasses. Her eyes and her long braids were two shades darker than her brown skin; she looked pretty, but also smart. And it wasn't just because of the blue glasses.

"That was weird on the bus yesterday," she announced suddenly.

I swallowed. "Yeah. It was."

"Why were those boys teasing you like that?"

"I really don't know."

She frowned. "If it was me, I wouldn't allow it."

"You think I *allowed* it?"

"I'm just saying, you don't have to put up with stuff like that, Mila. It's just really wrong, you know?"

Maybe I was reading too much into it, but it kind of felt like Samira was saying the whole bus thing was my fault.

"I didn't 'put up' with it, Samira," I said, my throat tight. "I told Dante to move and he refused. What else should I have done?"

At that moment Callum walked into the band room. Samira gave him a sideways look and flipped her braids over her shoulder.

Callum acted like he didn't notice either of us. He just walked over to his stand, raked his hair out of his eyes, took out his music and his trumpet, and began blowing scales. Loudly.

I wanted to ignore him the way he was ignoring Samira

and me, but it was impossible. He was so *there* in the band room, the sound of his trumpet just taking over. As if all the air molecules belonged to him.

And here was the strangest part: even though the way he was playing made me feel practically shoved out of the room, it was hard to think of him right then as a rude basketball boy, or one of the jerks on the bus. I mean, obviously, what happened yesterday had happened. Other people had seen it too—Samira, for example.

But listening to Callum play, seeing the sharp concentration in his eyes, I told myself that maybe, deep down, he wasn't like his stupid friends. He was a serious person. A real musician, who actually deserved to be trumpet section leader.

And according to Zara, Callum liked me, which I didn't think was true. But could it be possible? Because if Zara was right, it would almost explain why he acted this way— not starting the teasing, not doing very much of it himself, but going along with his dumb friends, so maybe they wouldn't guess the truth.

If it actually *was* the truth.

Which I doubted, anyway.

The bell rang for homeroom.

Samira sighed. "Well, I can't wait around for Ms. Fender," she said, almost to herself. "I'll just get the music later, I guess."

She picked up her backpack to leave the band room.

As I followed her out the door and into the hallway, I felt something brush against my back.

No, not my back. Lower than that.

"Hey, Mila," Callum murmured in my ear. His face was different now. Unserious. "You changed your outfit. Your butt looked nicer in that green sweater."

HOOPS

I think I may be coming down with something," I told Max. We were in the lunchroom, both of us getting chicken burritos with extra salsa.

Max sometimes acted like his brain had been watching YouTube instead of listening. "'Coming down with'?"

"Yeah, like I'm getting sick. Sickish. Anyway, I think maybe I'll just hang out in the library today, instead of going outside."

"But it's so nice out. And if you don't, we won't see you all day."

"I know, but . . ." I shrugged.

Suddenly Max looked at me through his long messy hair. Now he was definitely paying attention.

"Is it about those boys?" he asked.

I nibbled the burrito. "What boys?"

"You know. The boys who did that hug for Omi's birthday, and then that stuff on the blacktop yesterday. Especially Tobias—"

I swallowed. How much did Max know? He hadn't seen the hug in the band room, and he hadn't been on the bus yesterday either. And on the blacktop yesterday at lunch, he'd acted as if he hadn't even noticed anything.

But of course he would. Max was always on the lookout for teasing ever since last year, when Hunter Schultz called him "gay" and "Maxipad" and a bunch of other things. Until finally I convinced Max to tell Mr. McCabe, who made Hunter's parents come to school for a conference. For the whole rest of sixth grade, Hunter wasn't allowed within twenty feet of Max, and so far this year, he was keeping away. Still, I knew Max was jumpy.

"It's *sort* of about the boys," I admitted, licking salsa off my hand. "But also I have cramps."

I said this because Max always changed the subject whenever Omi, Zara, and I did period talk. But I guess he didn't believe me this time.

"Because you know I could help you," Max said as he grabbed a bunch of paper napkins and stuffed some into my hand. "Remember last year with Hunter? And how you wouldn't let me just hide in the library?"

"Of course I remember. And I'm not hiding—"

"Look, Mila, I'll come with you if you want to report them. We could do it right now."

"Thanks, but no," I said quickly. "And it's not like that, anyway. I mean, like how it was with you and Hunter. But really, thank you."

Max scowled as he chomped on an apple.

And now Omi and Zara were zooming toward us.

"Omigod, I'm so nervous I could barf!" Zara yelled. Today her tee said BE DANCED, OR DANCE. Which for a second almost made sense.

"They're having tryouts in chorus today," Omi explained. "For solos, right after lunch. And Zara, please save your barf for outside."

"I'll *try*," Zara said. "But let's hurry up and get out of here!" She clutched my arm with sweaty fingers. "Mila, say something positive."

"Okay, I'm *positive* you'll do great," I declared as I took a big messy bite of burrito.

"You are? Really? Tell me why!"

"Because you have a beautiful voice, and everyone knows it. And if you don't get a solo, I'll boycott the concert."

"So will I," Max said. "We'll carry signs—"

"We'll walk out of homeroom," Omi added.

Zara burst into nervous giggles. "You guys. You're the best. Just keep distracting me, okay? But only say *positive* stuff."

She was still clutching my arm as she led us out the lunchroom door onto the blacktop. I had to admit it felt great to be in the warm sunshine, not hiding by myself in the library. After all, who knew how many more nice, sunny days were left this fall? Already the nights were getting chilly, and leaves were starting to turn yellow and orange.

The four of us were headed over to our usual place—over by the pebbles—when all of a sudden Zara stopped. "Hey, you know what? I think I'll shoot hoops today."

"You mean play basketball?" I said. "With the boys?"

"Why not?" Zara was taller than all of them, and she was a good athlete. Really good, actually. "I'm just feeling so hyper right now! Maybe it'll help to burn off some energy."

"Okay, but I just . . . don't know if they'd play with a girl," I said.

Zara looked indignant. "Why wouldn't they?"

"I just . . . think they can be weird. About girls." My face was starting to heat up.

"Well, *I* don't think they're weird. And you're supposed to be *positive*, Mila, remember? Anyway, if I don't run around, I think I'll go nuts!"

"We could do something else," Max said. He shot me a look. "Maybe join that untag game—?"

"Good idea," I agreed quickly.

But Zara was already doing small jumps on the balls of

her feet, like she was warming up for basketball. "That tag game, or whatever it is, is extremely stupid," she told Max. "No one can even remember the rules. And only the nerds are doing it, anyway."

"Well, but I *am* a nerd, though," Max said. "And so is Jared."

"Jared who?" I asked.

"Whitman. He's new, and he's in orchestra. And taking Latin."

"Ah, so that means there are two of you now," Zara teased.

"Come on, Zara, we're not the *only* ones taking Latin!" Max was smiling and blushing.

Huh, I thought. *Max likes this new boy. As in,* likes. *Okay.*

Oh.

"Zara, if you want to play basketball, you totally should," Omi said. "Go ahead. We'll cheer for you."

"Well, thank *you,* Omi," Zara said. Not even glancing at me, she marched straight toward the hoop.

"I'm playing," she announced. "Whose team am I on?"

The basketball boys stared at her. Leo laughed.

"Who says you're playing?" Dante asked.

"Me," Zara said. "I do. And do I have to get Ms. Wardak over here? Because I totally will—"

"Nah." Leo wiped his hair out of his eyes. He looked at

Zara, up and down, in a way that made my stomach twist. "Anyway, you're tall enough."

"Of course I am! I'm five eight."

"Yeah, that's definitely what you are," Dante said. "*Tall.* And straight, like a stick." He held up his hand sideways.

Tobias grinned.

I tried to catch Zara's eye, but she looked away.

And if Leo heard Dante's comment, you couldn't tell. He kept talking to Zara. "But there's a problem. If *you* play, the teams will be uneven. So we need another girl."

"Not me," Omi said quickly. "I'm wearing the wrong shoes. And besides—"

"Mila," Leo said, fixing his pale greenish eyes on me. "We want Mila to play."

Tobias laughed. "Yeah. Mila. Even if she's not wearing The Sweater."

Callum didn't say a word as he dribbled the ball. *Thwump, thwump, thwump* against the blacktop.

The moths were awake now, and fluttering. Like they'd seen a giant light bulb.

"Shut up, Callum," I blurted.

He looked up, surprised. "I didn't say anything."

Not now. But you said something to me in the band room, didn't you? When you knew Ms. Fender and Samira couldn't hear it.

Zara's eyes were darting to the boys, then to me, then

to Leo. "What sweater? You mean that green one—?"

"I told you, Zara," I said desperately. "They have this crazy idea it gave them luck—"

"Although maybe it wasn't just *The Sweater*," Tobias said.

"Yeah, Mila, let's see if that shirt is lucky too," Dante said. "Hug time!"

He opened his arms and took a zombie step toward me.

"Stop," I hollered, stepping backward. "That isn't funny, Dante!"

The boys laughed. And now some other boys were watching from a few steps behind the foul line. Hunter Schultz and three of his horrible friends.

That was when I realized that Max and Omi had slipped away.

And that Zara's face had a hard look I'd never seen before. Directed at *me*.

"Well, Mila," she said in a not-best-friendly voice. "If you don't want to play, no one is forcing you."

GUIDANCE

I speed-walked into the building, my chest pounding, no idea where I was even going. My friends had deserted me—why? Well, Max I could understand: he was scared of Hunter and his friends, and possibly of the basketball boys, too. And of course, when he'd offered to come with me to report them, I'd said no. Omi had followed Max off the blacktop, maybe to be loyal to Max, maybe to avoid watching things get weird between Zara and me. Knowing Omi, the way she tried to avoid every conflict, it was probably a little of both, I thought.

As for Zara, I didn't know what to think.

How come she didn't protest when the boys started teasing me? Sure, she was nervous about the chorus thing, but she couldn't have needed to play basketball that badly. And maybe she didn't know the whole story—the lie about Leo's birthday, the stuff on the bus, what happened with Callum this morning in the band room—but she'd seen a sample of it just now, happening right before her eyes, and she didn't take my side. Or even say *anything*. Not even when Dante called her "straight like a stick," which he'd obviously meant as an insult.

And why had she given me that strange look? Could she be jealous?

But of what? The boys' attention—including Leo's—was the opposite of flattering. I couldn't understand how Zara didn't see that, or get how awful this was for me.

Does she care more about Leo than about my feelings?

It was hard to believe. But also the only thing that made any sense.

I checked my phone: twenty-one minutes until band. Ms. Wardak was out on the blacktop, so she couldn't yell at me for being in the hallway. Still, I knew I probably couldn't just hang out here for the next twenty-one minutes without anyone noticing. Better to look as if I had a Place to Be.

I wandered down the main corridor, until I found myself in front of the door marked GUIDANCE.

Actually, that's exactly what I do need. Guidance.

Not to tattle on anyone, like a baby. Besides, the way

Zara acted just now, if I got Leo in trouble, she'd probably never speak to me again. And then neither would Omi, most likely.

But it would be good to get some advice. Also to know how to think about the last few days. The letter with my homeroom assignment had said that my guidance counselor was named Lori Maniscalco; from what I could tell at the assembly two weeks ago, when all the seventh grade counselors introduced themselves, she seemed really nice. Like you could imagine telling her things.

I walked up to a woman sitting behind a desk. She had drawn-on eyebrows and hair that sat on her head at a weird angle. I couldn't help staring; a second too late, after she noticed I was staring, I realized it was a wig.

I read her name plaque: MS. J. KURTZBURGER.

"Hello, Ms. Kurtzburger," I said, working hard to keep my voice steady. "My name is Mila Brennan, and I'd like to talk to Ms. Maniscalco. Please. It's very important."

Ms. Kurtzburger looked up from her monitor. "Oh, I'm sorry, but Ms. Maniscalco isn't here. Haven't you heard? She's on maternity leave."

She was? At the assembly, when she'd waddled up to the mic, I could see she was pregnant. But I hadn't thought she was *that* pregnant.

I couldn't help it; I burst into tears.

Ms. Kurtzburger got up from her seat and handed me

a box of tissues on which someone (Ms. Kurtzburger?) had written in Sharpie: GUIDANCE. DO NOT MOVE.

She sat again and quickly typed something on her keyboard. "Hold on, Mila. Let me check something for you. Okay, we don't have a maternity-leave replacement lined up for Ms. Maniscalco quite yet, so until we do, you can talk to Mr. Dolan."

"Mr. Dolan? I don't even know him!"

I knew it sounded stupid to be making this argument, because it wasn't as if I knew Mrs. Maniscalco, either. But the truth was, if I'd known I'd be talking to *Mr.* Anybody, I wouldn't have come here. I needed Ms. Maniscalco, who'd seemed so understanding and . . . *a woman.*

"Well, let's just see if he's available." Ms. Kurtzburger rose again and knocked on a door a few feet down the hall. "Okay if I send in Mila Brennan? One of Lori's."

"Sure!" a cheerful male voice boomed into the hallway.

Still time to escape, I told myself. *Just go!*

But I walked down the hall and into Mr. Dolan's tiny office. He was a young, thick-looking man with a buzz cut and a school ring. On his walls were signed posters of baseball players, and his small gray sofa had a blue-and-orange pillow that said CHICAGO BEARS.

"How may I help you today?" Mr. Dolan asked. His eyes were crinkled, and he was smiling.

Run!

"Um," I said. "Actually, I was hoping to see Ms. Maniscalco. I didn't know she'd be leaving—"

"Neither did she! But baby Ryan decided to make an early appearance." He grinned. "So what's going on? *Mila*," he added, to show that he knew my name.

My throat felt as if I'd swallowed glass. Or maybe pebbles. "It's a little hard to talk about."

"But that's what you're here for, right? So why not try me." He gestured toward the sofa.

By now I was trapped. So I perched on the edge of the thin foam sofa cushion. "Okay. Well. Actually, I'm being teased. Sort of."

"Sort of teased, or teased?"

"Well, it's not regular teasing."

"How so?"

"It's hard to explain."

"Okay," Mr. Dolan said. "I'm sorry to hear this, Mila. Can I ask by who?"

"I'd rather not give out names."

"Fair enough. Although that does make my job harder." He leaned one elbow on the arm of his swivel chair and rested his cheek on his fist. This was obviously his listening face. "Can you tell me anything *about* the kids doing the teasing?"

"Not really." I cleared my throat.

"Well, Mila, it's a little difficult—"

"They're boys."

"Gotcha. And what are these boys teasing you about? If you don't mind telling me."

"Um. My clothes."

"Your clothes?" He glanced at my red tablecloth shirt.

"Yeah, basically," I said.

"Are they saying anything in particular?"

"No. Just about . . . my clothes."

He nodded slowly. "Okay, Mila. I guess you understand that when there's a conflict, normally what I do is bring all the kids involved into my office, have a friendly sit-down, talk it over, and work things out. But if a student tells me she doesn't want to identify all the parties to the conflict—"

"I'd rather not."

"—then it's a little hard for me to help. You understand that, Mila?"

By this time, I was getting annoyed with how often he said the word *Mila*. Like maybe he thought if he repeated my name enough times, he'd hypnotize me into trusting him better.

"I guess," I said.

"So here's the best I can do, under the circumstances. You're aware, I bet, that seventh grade boys can be very immature. They act like big shots, some of them, but they can say some gross and stupid things. And the truth is, they'll pretty much tease anyone or anything that moves."

Yes, but I know what teasing is. This is different.

Mr. Dolan leaned toward me; his swivel chair squeaked. "It doesn't mean these boys are gross and stupid *inside*; mostly they're just showing off for their friends. So if that's what's going on, Mila, I can tell you from experience that the best course of action is to try to ignore them."

But that's impossible. They won't let me ignore them!

I nodded.

"Ignoring isn't easy, I know." He smiled. "But I promise you, it can be very effective."

"Okay. I'll try."

"Good." Now Mr. Dolan rose, dusting off invisible crumbs from his pants. "Well, Mila, I'm always right here if you want to chat. Let me know how things go, okay?"

I got up too. "I will," I said. "Thank you. Um."

"Yes, Mila?"

I felt my face on fire. "Do you know when Ms. Maniscalco will be back?"

"You mean back from maternity leave?"

"Yeah. Yes."

"Three months," Mr. Dolan answered.

CHAIRS

Ms. Fender was standing in the hallway outside the band room, chatting with Mr. Broadwater, the orchestra teacher. Which meant she wasn't inside the band room. Which meant I didn't want to go inside the band room either.

So I hung out in front of the band room door, tying my sneaker laces. Then untying them. Then triple-knotting them.

Ugh. They're so dirty and frayed. I really need to ask Mom to buy me new laces. Maybe if we go shopping this weekend, like she promised. Although she said she might have to work—

Finally Ms. Fender noticed me. "Mila? You should be inside, warming up. I'll be there in a second."

"Oh, okay," I said.

Please, please hurry.

I crossed the buzzing band room. Some kids were doing scales, some were getting their music arranged on their stands, but most were chatting and laughing. I took my seat next to Callum, who was leaning behind him to say something to Dante.

I took my trumpet out of its case. It looked smudgy, so I wiped it with the little gray cloth. *Wipe, wipe, wipe.* Wiping was fascinating and important.

"Hey, Mila," Callum said.

Wipe, wipe, wipe.

"Mila."

Wipe—

"*Mila.* Where did you go at lunch?"

"How is that your business?"

"It's not. Are you mad at us?"

Wipe.

"Please don't be mad, okay? We were just fooling around."

"You should really have a sense of humor," Dante said.

Oh, so he was in this conversation too?

"For your information, I *do* have a sense of humor," I said. "A *great* one, in fact. But that stupid hug business isn't funny. I'm getting really sick of it, and I want you to stop, okay? All of you. Including Leo and Tobias."

"Okay," Callum said.

What?

He said okay.

That was it? All I had to do was say the word "stop," and then he'd say "okay," and then all this horrible not-just-teasing stuff would be over? And now everything would be going back to normal, at lunch and with my friends?

It was almost too good to believe!

Why hadn't I figured this out before?

As I put away my cloth and set up "Pirate Medley" on my music stand, I couldn't stop grinning. THE WEIRD-NESS WAS OVER NOW. HALLELUJAH!

And then I noticed that Callum's chair had inched closer to mine. Maybe he hadn't even realized it.

Whatever. I definitely wasn't going to start a fight with him about floor space now that he'd agreed to stop being a jerk. I scooched my chair six inches to the right.

"Hey," Rowan Crawley protested. "You're crowding, Mila."

"I am? Sorry."

I scooched back to the left. Not all the way, though. Four inches.

Callum studied his music. And I thought: *The best thing about him is that serious face.*

At last Ms. Fender walked to the front of the room. "All right, guys. Musician posture: backs straight, chests open, feet on the floor, eyes on me. Let's take 'Pirate Medley' from rehearsal letter B. I want to hear crisp, clear notes and a steady beat. Samira, would you please play the first two measures—"

Pet Number One rose from her chair to play.

A few seconds passed as we all listened to Samira's clarinet.

And then I became aware of something behind my head. It was a feeling like when there's a mosquito buzzing around you in the dark: you can't see it, but you have this general sense of *annoying bug* somewhere around your body.

The back of my neck tingled; I reached behind to grab my ponytail.

And my hand smacked into something.

Dante's nose.

"Ow!" he yelled, falling backward.

I gaped. "What were you doing?"

"Nothing," Dante said. He rubbed his nostrils.

"You guys," Annabel Cho whispered loudly. "Shut up! Samira is playing—"

Dante ignored her. "I just forgot my music, Mila, so I was leaning over to read yours."

"I don't believe you!" I hissed.

"Well, you should," Callum said. "Dante is a very truthful person."

On either side of Dante, Luis Garcia and Daniel Chun

were snickering. Annabel was scowling, and two seats over, Liana Brock was making her face go blank, as if she hadn't seen anything, which was totally impossible.

A cold wave of sweat passed over my body.

How is this happening?! I thought we just agreed that this stuff was over.

And why hasn't anyone stopped it? Luis, Daniel, Annabel, Liana—

Samira finished playing. The way she took her chair and huffed, you could tell she was annoyed by the disruption.

So was Ms. Fender. "Is there a problem over in the trumpet section?" she demanded. "Some reason to be rude to a fellow musician?"

It took me a second to realize that by "fellow musician" Ms. Fender meant Samira, not me.

"Sorry," I said. "Dante was crowding my chair just now."

"I didn't mean to," Dante insisted. "I was just trying to read the music. And Mila didn't need to react like that anyway."

"Overreact," Callum said.

Ms. Fender crossed her arms. "Dante, please explain to me why you needed to read Mila's music."

Yeah. Go ahead. I'm listening.

"Because I left mine in my locker. By accident," Dante added. He looked embarrassed.

"Well, I expect you to come to band fully prepared,"

Ms. Fender scolded. "And if you folks can't respect a band member when she's playing, and you can't sit still in your chairs without acting like kindergartners, then we'll need to make some changes. Am I being clear?"

It sounded like she was including me, like she thought *I* was one of the kindergartners. I could feel my cheeks burn.

"Sorry," I said again.

"Sorry," Dante repeated.

Callum made his serious-musician face. "It won't happen again, Ms. Fender."

"Well, good," she said, pressing her lips.

Maybe Ms. Fender believed that, but I sure didn't.

SNEAKERS

So that was how I knew that it wasn't over.

I mean, if nothing else had happened these past few days, I might have thought Dante's excuse was believable. But even if he'd left his music in his locker by accident, he didn't need to read *my* music; he could have looked on with Daniel or Luis. Or he could have peeked over Callum, who was actually his friend.

Also, Dante wasn't blind; if he was really reading off my music stand, he didn't need to have his face practically *in my hair*. Not to mention the fact that he could have tapped me on the shoulder or something, to ask if I minded him sitting so close.

Plus, the way Callum had been scooching over—at the time, I wasn't positive it was happening, but now, looking back, I knew it was. Even though he'd told me, *Okay, Mila, we'll stop doing whatever we're doing*, it was as if he'd said: *Actually, on second thought? Nothing has changed. And nothing you do will make any difference.*

Talking to us. Or not talking to us.

Ignoring us. Or not ignoring us.

Oh, and the bus home? Don't take it if you don't want more trouble.

So when the bell rang for dismissal, I didn't even consider getting on. The thought of sitting next to Dante or any of the others, getting shoulder-bumped, or crowded, or squeezed when I got off, having the creepy mosquito-near-my-head feeling again—it just wasn't *possible*. The walk home was about two miles, but I was wearing sneakers. I needed to be home in time for Hadley's bus, but if I moved fast enough, I could make it okay.

I mean, probably. Unless her bus got there extra early.

I gave my old and dirty laces one last retie, buttoned my tablecloth shirt up to the top, and started walking.

LATE

When I got home, Hadley was sitting on our front stoop with Cherish Ames, a kindergartner on our block who still sucked her thumb, and Cherish's mom, who had dyed-blond hair that reached down to her waist. I mean, it was nice, but definitely strange-looking for mom hair.

As soon as she saw me, Cherish's mom stood, swishing her hair. "Well, there she is! See?" she said to Hadley. "I told you Mila hadn't forgotten!"

"Why would I forget to come home?" I asked. Did that sound fresh? I wasn't sure.

"Well, honey, you're four minutes late." Cherish's mom did a smile at me that was all teeth. "And Hadley was *extremely* worried."

I glanced at my sister. She was eating Oreos—not the cheap kind Mom bought (which I called Store-eos) but the real kind. Cherish's mom must have packed them in her bag, maybe to distract Cherish from thumb-sucking.

"Well, I had to stay after school to finish a project," I lied. "But thanks for sitting with Hadley."

"No problem. But Mila, next time you have a project"— she said the word in quotation marks, as if she could tell it was a lie—"please call me, so I'll know to watch out for Hadley. Can I have your phone? I'll put my number in your contacts."

She held out her hand. So it wasn't a choice: I gave her my phone, and she entered her number with blue-polished fingertips.

Then she gave it back to me and, in one motion, yanked Cherish's thumb from her mouth.

"Not in public, muffin," she said in a drippy voice. "Okay, bye, Hadley honey."

"Bye," Hadley said.

I opened our front door with my key. The two of us went inside, and Hadley sat down in the dinette.

I got some milk from the fridge and poured myself a glass. "You want some?"

Hadley shook her head, but I gave her a glass anyway.

"What kind of a name is Cherish?" I said. "It's like naming

someone Mommy Loves You. No wonder that kid still sucks her thumb."

Normally, Hadley would giggle, at the very least. Now she just shrugged.

"And what kind of mom has hair like that?" I continued. "I'm sure glad Mom doesn't look like an old teenager. Aren't you, Had?"

Hadley shrugged again.

I sighed. "Okay. So are you mad at me?"

"Yeah," Hadley said.

I sat at the table. "Well, I'm very sorry. I had to stay late at school. It wasn't my choice."

"You had a project?"

"Sort of, yeah."

"What's it on?"

"It's complicated. Anyway, if I ever have another project, I'll call Mrs. Ames, so you don't have to worry. And next time I'll get home faster, I promise."

"Okay," Hadley said. She didn't sound super convinced.

I watched as she drank her milk to the bottom of the glass.

Then I said, "Hadley? Can you do me a huge, huge favor? Can you not tell Mom I was late?"

"You mean not tell her about your project?"

"Yeah."

"How come?"

"Well, because she's so stressed about her job these days, isn't she? She's always talking about her mean boss. And I don't want her to worry about me."

Hadley frowned. "Why would she worry about you?"

"Oh, because she worries about everything! And she's so tired when she gets home. We just need to let her relax, okay?"

Hadley's face scrunched up, and for a second I thought she was going to cry. But then I realized it was a dog-sniffing face.

And suddenly she got up from the table and ran into the living room.

"Eww, gross," she shouted. "Delilah had an accident!"

PARK

After that long walk home, the absolute last thing I wanted to do right then was walk Delilah. But not walking her wouldn't be fair; it wasn't *her* fault I couldn't take the bus. Or that I was late, and she'd had the accident.

So after cleaning up the mess, I told Hadley I was taking Delilah to Deamer Park to run off leash, which was her favorite thing ever. And of course if Delilah and I were going, Hadley had to come too.

"Well, okayyy," Hadley said. Like, *I'm still mad at you, Mila, so you'd better be nice to me, or I'll tell.*

But as soon as we were out the door, she was her old self again, chatting nonstop about a kid in her class who lost a tooth and got ten dollars from the Tooth Fairy. And then his big brother asked him if he believed there was really a Tooth Fairy, and when he said no, the brother said he should return the money.

There was way more to this story, but after a while I zoned out, letting Hadley go on and on, just adding "Huh" and "Uh-huh" whenever she paused. Mostly I was watching the people on the street step into stores and check their mail and feed the parking meter. And I can't explain why, but after all the weirdness today, seeing all this normal, boring stuff was sort of comforting.

It was like: You know those camera shots where there's this goldfish swimming in a little bowl, and then the camera pulls back and you realize the bowl is actually a pond? And then it pulls back again, so you can see the pond is really the ocean? And then the camera keeps zooming out, farther and farther, until you see all the oceans and continents on Planet Earth?

I always liked that camera stuff, because to me it was saying that all your problems—the swimming-in-the-goldfish-bowl stuff—were really small and unimportant compared to the entire world. And walking with Hadley and Delilah that day, seeing everything that happened on a regular afternoon, it was kind of a version of that wide camera shot, reminding me of all the things in existence that were Not-School.

Which was a surprisingly long list, actually, I thought as we passed the library, the post office, my favorite pizza place, the urgent-care building, a real-estate office, a building with a new sign that said E MOTIONS. For a block or two, my brain played with that: What were they selling in there? Embarrassment? Jealousy? No, because who'd want that?

Can I please have a quarter pound of Happiness? With a dash of Relief? No, make that two dashes, please. And an order of Surprise to go.

Finally we arrived at the entrance of Deamer Park. And then my heart stopped, because there, under a red maple tree, was Tobias. He was with a small curly-haired girl in purple overalls who looked like she was about two years old, and he was holding her hand.

"No ice cream, Bella," he was saying. "Too close to supper."

I froze. He hadn't noticed me yet.

"Why'd you stop?" Hadley protested. "Delilah's all excited. She wants to go in!"

Our dog was on her hind legs, straining toward the dog run, whimpering.

"Wanna pet that doggie," the little girl announced. She pointed a finger at Delilah.

"*Oh,*" Tobias said, when he realized who Delilah was attached to. A blush began creeping up his neck. "Hi, Mila."

"Hi," I said. "It's okay if she wants to pet her. My dog is friendly."

Immediately I was furious at myself: Why had I said this? It was like a stupid reflex:

Other person: Ooh, nice dog. Can I pet her?

Me (proud dog owner): Sure!

And maybe I could have followed up with a line like: *Tobias, as long as we're having a normal conversation, why do you keep acting like such a jerk?* Or: *Stop teasing me at school, because it's horrible and I don't like it.* Or even: *Keep your hands off me, Tobias, and tell your stupid friends, too!*

But I didn't say anything. For three reasons.

First, because I was with Hadley. I'd already asked her not to tell Mom about my being late; I couldn't *also* ask her to keep quiet about the boy thing.

Second, because the little girl, who I guessed was Tobias's sister, began smooshing Delilah's ears, which made Delilah wag her tail, and then lean against Tobias in total love with him. Which made Tobias start crooning stuff like "good girl" and "nice doggie" while his little sister squealed with delight. So yelling at him would have been kind of awkward.

And third, because ten seconds later a curly-haired woman walked out of the playground loudly scolding a boy around Hadley's age.

"When I say it's time to leave, *no arguments*, Sam," the woman told the boy. Then she spotted Tobias and Bella. And Hadley, Delilah, and me.

She snatched Bella's hand from Delilah's head. Bella immediately started howling.

"Bell, we *never* pet strange dogs," the woman said sharply. "Tobias, did you ask—?"

Obviously, this was Tobias's mom. So I could have said, *No, actually, he didn't!*

And you want to hear what else he didn't ask?

But this woman was cranky, clearly in no mood to listen. *And anyhow,* I thought, *tattling to his mom would probably backfire.*

"It's okay," I said, avoiding Tobias's eyes. "I told them my dog is friendly."

"Even so, Bell, we keep our hands to ourselves," Tobias's mom said.

DOGS

Hadley and I sat on a rickety old bench in the dog run, watching Delilah zoom through the leaves with three other dogs. *It must be great to be a dog,* I thought. *You make friends with everyone, just like that. And if another dog gets in your face, you growl and right away the other dog backs off. It's all so incredibly . . . simple.*

"Hey, Mila, you know what?" Hadley said after a minute. "That was the kid."

"What kid?" I asked.

"The kid I was telling you about before. Who lost his tooth."

"Okay," I said. "But which kid are you referring to, specifically? This park is full of kids."

"I mean the kid we saw! *Sam.* Whose mom didn't like Delilah."

I stared at my little sister. "Wait, what? You mean just now, at the entrance—"

Hadley nodded.

"Why didn't you say hello, if you knew him?"

"Because."

"Huh," I said, as if that made any sense. "So I guess that older boy was his mean big brother."

"What mean big brother?"

Sometimes my little sister was impossible to have a conversation with. "Hadley, weren't you telling me a whole long story on the walk over here about how that kid Sam's big brother said if he didn't believe in the Tooth Fairy he had to return the ten dollars—"

"Yeah, but it was a joke."

"A joke? I don't get it."

"Mila, weren't you *listening*?" Hadley sighed impatiently. "I said Sam *tried* to give his brother the money, but his brother said no! He was only *joking*!"

"Oh," I said.

Of all the things I wanted in my brain right then, the absolute last was Tobias Segal as a big brother. But I couldn't help it. The way he was holding his little sister's hand, explaining about ice cream, the way he smooshed

Delilah's ears—really, it was a different side of his personality. The non-jerk side.

Sort of like Callum's non-jerk side when he was playing trumpet. And maybe Dante's when he was being a computer genius.

And then I thought:

> Maybe all the basketball boys have
> non-jerk sides, including Leo.
> They probably have moms who teach them
> not to touch strange dogs,
> and little brothers they tease,
> but just enough.
> And when it comes to taking their Tooth
> Fairy money,
> they know exactly when to stop.
> So why is it different when it comes to me?

MOM

Where have you guys been?" Mom shouted as soon as we walked in the door. Her face was flushed and her eyes were pink and swollen. Right away I could tell she'd been crying.

"Mom, are you okay?" I asked.

"I'm fine! Just a little upset about some stuff going on at work. Don't worry about it." She blew her nose. "But Mila, I told you I was getting home early for my exercise class tonight! And when I got home, no one was here; there's no note, nobody texted, so I had no idea *where* you were. And nothing's defrosted for supper—"

Ugh. "Sorry, Mom," I said. "This whole day has been really crazy. We were just at the dog run—"

"Delilah pooped in the living room," Hadley cut in. "It was stinky. So we thought she needed extra time at the park. Also we saw this kid in my class called Sam. Who got ten dollars for losing a tooth."

I flashed my sister a grateful look. She hadn't said anything about how I was late.

"Well, you'll just have to come with me, then," Mom said. Now she was stuffing some exercise clothes in a plastic Kohl's bag. "My class starts in fourteen minutes. It's an hour long, and afterward we'll go out to eat."

"Ooh, Mommy, can we go to Junior Jay's for supper?" Hadley squealed. "Please, please, please?"

Junior Jay's had vanilla shakes and onion rings. If my sister could eat nothing else for the rest of her life, she'd be perfectly okay with that.

Mom kissed Hadley's cheek. "Yes, baby, we can. But only if you're quiet while I have my class. No running around the halls, and you have to listen to Mila."

"Wait," I said. "I have to come too? To watch Hadley? But Mom, I have homework—"

"So bring it with you. You can sit with Hadley in the hallway."

"But that's not fair!" I exploded. "Why do I have to watch Hadley all the time! And walk Delilah! And make supper—"

Mom looked shocked. "Mila, you know I count on you for help."

94

"Yes, but what about *me*?" Suddenly my eyes were full of tears. "How come no one ever thinks about what *I* want?"

"Oh, sweetheart," Mom said. She threw her arms around me. And then she started crying all over again.

So I threw my arms around her, and we both stood there crying into each other's hair. What were we both crying about? I sort of knew why I was, and it had nothing to do with math homework, or even watching my sister. But I had no idea about Mom. She'd cried at movies in front of us, but never at anything real. Was this about her job? Or maybe another fight on the phone with Dad?

Hadley grabbed both of us around the waist and squeezed tight. The three of us hugged like that for almost a whole minute.

"I'm so sorry, Mila," Mom said into my hair. "You're right. I do expect an awful lot of you. Maybe too much. I should have asked if you were okay with this."

I pulled away to get us both some napkins off the dinette table. "It's fine. I'll bring my math book. I know you really want to do this class."

"I don't want to—I *need* to. I'm feeling so out of shape lately!"

"Mommy, you're a beautiful shape," Hadley declared.

"Thanks, baby. I just mean I haven't exercised in a while." Mom's laugh seemed a little forced, I thought. "So anyway, are we ready? E Motions is just downtown, but if we're going out to eat right afterward, let's take the car—"

"E Motions?" I said. "You mean that new place?"

Mom nodded. "They just opened, so there's this introductory deal where all sessions are free for your first two weeks. That's why I want to go. They have all sorts of cool classes—yoga, hip-hop, karate—"

I'll have some Happiness. And a dash of Relief.

And maybe a sprinkle of Anger.

No, two sprinkles.

E MOTIONS

By the time we got downtown, and Mom found a parking spot, and the three of us walked into E Motions, Mom was two minutes late for her exercise class. She told Hadley and me to sit in the front reception area, which was basically just three metal folding chairs and a small table that had magazines I'd never heard of before with titles like *You* and *Yourself*. Not exactly my kind of reading, so I opened my math book.

Hadley poked me. "What should I do, Mila?"

"I don't know," I said. "Did you bring any homework?" I pointed to her pink backpack.

"We just had a dot-to-dot and practicing the letter *M*, but I did those on the bus."

"Well, look at the magazines, then. Find words you can read."

She opened *Yourself.* "They, go, but, not, you, was, walk." She closed it. "I'm boooored."

"Had, you can't be bored. We just got here!"

"Excuse me," said a woman who'd just entered the waiting area. She was small and blond, in a neon green tank top that said E MOTIONS! LET'S GET MOVING! Her arms were super muscled; I tried not to stare, but I'd never seen a woman with arms like that. "Did someone just say the word 'bored'?"

"I did," Hadley answered, actually raising her hand.

"Well, we can't have that, can we?" The woman grinned. Her teeth were incredibly white. "I'm Erica, the owner. I had a manager until yesterday, but she quit. Sorry there was no one here to greet you."

E Motions. Named for Erica. Okay, now I get it.

"Oh, we didn't need a greeting," I said.

"Well, I just want everyone to feel welcome." Erica reached out her hand to shake ours. Her grip was firmer than I was expecting. "So are you guys here with someone?"

"Our mom, but she's in a exercise class because she's out of a shape," Hadley said.

I shot my sister a look. "We're just here for an hour. And we'll be quiet now, I promise."

"Well, why be quiet when you can have fun?" Erica said. "Either of you girls like dancing? We have a cool class going on right now."

Hadley jumped up. Literally jumped. "I loooove to dance! I dance *all the time!*"

"No you don't," I told her.

Erica nodded at me. "What about you? Do you like to dance?"

"Me? Oh no. Not at all. And I have math to do, so." I held up my book.

"Well, what I always find is that when you take a break and move some muscles, it helps stimulate those brain cells." She did a little dance-step sort of thing. It was so dorky I had to look away. "That's how it works for me, anyway."

"Okay," I said, trying to keep my voice as polite as possible.

"Well, all right, then," Erica said cheerfully. "So would it be okay if your little sister has a peek at our hip-hop class? It's just down the hall. I'll have her back here in a few minutes."

"Please, Mila?" Hadley begged, jumping. *"Pleeeease?"*

"Oh, she can stay the whole hour," I said immediately.

BOW

I did math for the next fifteen minutes, finishing all but two problems, which I knew I'd never get even if I worked on them all night. So I closed the textbook and stood to stretch my legs. Then I walked around the reception area three times.

How was Hadley doing in that dance class? *Just fine, probably,* I answered myself, because if she weren't, Erica or someone would be bringing her out here again. But Mom was expecting that I'd literally watch my little sister, not hand her over to the E Motions owner, so maybe I should check.

I walked down the hall, listening to teachers in all the different rooms.

"Take a deep cleansing breath . . . and another. And now . . . downward-facing dog into eagle pose . . ."

"And toe! And toe! And *step*, two, three!"

"Work those back muscles, people! I want to see perfect, upright posture!"

"Kiai!"

The last voice was high and sharp. It didn't sound like a teacher's.

I peeked inside room 5. About twenty kids of different sizes and ages, girls and boys, were standing with their backs to me, facing a young woman with very short, reddish-purplish hair. All the students wore white uniforms, but they had different-colored belts—mostly white or yellow, but a few of them were orange or green. The young woman, who was clearly the teacher, had a black belt.

"Let's hear that again, Ms. Carter," she was telling one student. "'Kiai' is Japanese for 'spirit yell,' so don't hold back. Yell out as you exhale."

"But I'm supposed to be falling," the girl said. She had a white belt, and seemed younger than me, so it was weird to hear her called *Ms.* Anything. "And I thought the kiai was what you say when you're attacking."

"Yes, but the yell is also meant to draw attention," the teacher said. "You *want* people to look, *especially* if you're vulnerable. Plus it unnerves the attacker. You don't have to say 'kiai'—some people say 'ha,' or 'hey,' or a different word. The important thing is to let your spirit yell out. And not from high up in the throat but from deep, from the stomach. Try again, Ms. Carter."

The girl threw herself on the shiny blue mat, yelling "kiai" so loudly this time that I flinched.

"Nice job!" The teacher high-fived the girl, who beamed.

It was so dramatic that at first I didn't register someone calling my name. And then I realized that a girl with an orange belt had gotten off the mat and was coming toward me. Her long braids were coiled in a bun, and she wasn't wearing blue glasses—so it took me a second to recognize Samira.

"Hey, Mila, you're doing this class?" she was asking. She seemed surprised, with maybe a dash of happy.

"Me? No," I said, blushing. "My mom is here, and my little sister . . ." I waved my arm in the direction of the hip-hop class.

Now the teacher was walking over. "Welcome," she said. "My name is Ms. Platt. I'm the head teacher here. And you're . . . ?"

"Oh, no. I was just watching."

"Even so, I take it you have a name?" Ms. Platt smiled.

"Mila."

"Mila, you need to bow," Samira said.

Bow? Was she serious?

I lowered my head and bent over like I had a stomach cramp.

Ms. Platt smiled and bowed back. Not the sort of bow musicians did: this one was heels together, arms at the side, eyes straight ahead, bending at the waist.

"Mila what?" she asked when she finished bowing.

"Brennan."

"Well, you're welcome to join us, Ms. Brennan, or even just to keep observing. But in this dojo we do ask that you remove your shoes."

My shoes? She meant my sneakers, which I'd been wearing this entire crazy day—to school, on the long walk home, then to the dog run. Suddenly I couldn't think of anything I'd rather do than take off my filthy, stinky sneakers. And hanging out in this class would kill some time while I waited for Mom and Hadley.

I crouched to unknot my frayed, triple-knotted laces. What about socks? I peeked: all the other kids had bare feet, so I took off my socks and stuck them inside my sneakers.

And now you can't escape, my brain scolded me. *Not too sure this is your best idea, Mila.*

"Aswatte," Ms. Platt told the class. She looked at me. "Ms. Brennan, I just asked the students to sit. Have you studied karate or other martial arts before?"

I shook my head.

"Please say, 'No, sensei,'" Ms. Platt said. "It means 'teacher' in Japanese."

Why did she care what I called her? I wasn't even supposed to be here.

My cheeks were burning. But I said it.

Ms. Platt bowed her head. "This is not a pure karate class, Ms. Brennan—we incorporate several martial arts. But we do use a little Japanese, so if you don't understand something, always feel free to ask."

"Thanks." *Okay, leave! Now! You don't have to stay here out of politeness or embarrassment. Just pick up your sneakers and RUN.*

I crossed the floor to the edge of the blue mat where kids were sitting with crossed legs, watching silently as Samira and two girls in yellow belts did a bunch of movements. Ms. Platt was standing beside them, doing the same movements and sort of narrating: "Okay, begin with the heiko-dachi stance, step back with the right foot, catch to the back leg, overhead block with the left hand, straight-forward punch with the right hand, pull the block in. Kiai. Heiko-dachi. Again, please."

Then Ms. Platt asked them to "demonstrate Basic Seven," and the whole class followed along while counting out loud in Japanese.

I couldn't take my eyes off Samira and the other girls—

they seemed so sure of themselves, and focused. Like Samira when she played clarinet, and Callum when he played trumpet. And even like Zara sometimes, when she was singing.

But also, this was different, because of the way they were using their bodies. The sharp, clean movements with no hesitation. Not just punching, but also blocking. And then that wild spirit yell at the end.

Which possibly was their sort of blue sky.

And I thought:

How do you get like that?
Knowing what to do, in what order.
Not thinking. Or not-thinking.
Not ignoring. And not running away.
Could I ever do any of that?
Could one of those girls ever be me?
As hard as I tried, it was impossible to
imagine.

MAYBE

The whole drive over to Junior Jay's, and then the whole meal, Hadley wouldn't stop talking about the hip-hop class, how much fun it was, how she really, really, *really* wanted to go again, and could she please get purple leggings like the dance teacher had, *pleeease*?

Mom just let her talk, because she knew that once Hadley got started, there was no point interrupting. Finally she said, "Well, baby, you can go for the next two weeks, but after the introductory offer, E Motions isn't free. And I wish I was sure we could afford their classes, but I don't know yet. Maybe."

Hadley slurped her milkshake. "Maybe means maybe yes, right?"

"Had, it also means maybe no," I said.

"But just as much yes! Maybe yes *or* no, but it *could* be yes, right, Mommy?"

Mom made a *shhh* finger at Hadley. "Restaurant voices, please. Maybe means . . . well, let's not count any chickens, girls, but it's possible I *might* be getting a raise. I'm not sure about it, but I have a meeting scheduled to discuss it, and I'm hoping. And if I do get it, we'll have a little breathing room in our budget."

"That's great, Mom," I said.

Although the truth was, I was shocked. After the way Mom had been crying when Hadley and I got home from the dog run—which she'd blamed on "stuff at work"—I didn't understand how she could be getting a raise. Was work going okay, or wasn't it? If it was, why had she been so upset?

It sort of felt like yesterday, when I came home from school and studied myself in the mirror, wondering what the boys saw when they looked at me.

Sometimes you could look at something right up close and still not know what you were seeing.

COVERAGE

When my alarm rang on Friday morning, the first thing I noticed was that on the end of my bed was a neat stack of clothes. Mom clothes, which she must have picked for me. Not worky outfits, but the things she wore on weekends—a loose white sweater with tiny pills, a tee that said UNIVERSITY OF LIFE, another big flannel shirt I'd never seen before, in a pale blue plaid, with a metal button at the collar that didn't match the others. Could I seriously wear any of this grown-up stuff to school?

I picked up the white sweater with the tiny pills. It smelled like laundry detergent and mom perfume. Okay, maybe not.

And that tee—omigod, no way. Only Zara did the funny-tee thing, and all of hers were bad translations from the internet. This was mom humor, and just not funny.

Although the plaid shirt wasn't awful. But plaid two days in a row? That might seem strange, like suddenly I'd morphed into this Plaid-Wearing Person.

On the other hand, I told myself, *so what?* The shirt was worn-looking, with a mismatched button, but it wouldn't cling, or give out too much information. It would be long enough to cover my butt, and there was plenty of room across the chest. So in those two ways, it would be perfect, really.

And then I had this thought: Does Mom *know* this about me? That I need coverage?

I wondered how she knew this, if she actually did.

TURQUOISE

I have this memory:

I am almost seven years old, in second grade. All my friends and I are obsessed with these animated tigers called Ti-grrlz, which are suddenly everywhere: on TV, clothes, backpacks, stickers. There's even a Ti-grrlz series of chapter books, and I've read every one at least three times.

There are six different Ti-grrlz, named for the color of their stripes: Pink, Purple, Blue, Green, Yellow, and Turquoise. My favorite is Turquoise. I draw her all over my spelling notebook and get in trouble with my teacher.

February 19 is my birthday, more than a year since I last saw Dad, and this time he doesn't even send a present. Mom knows I'm feeling sad about that, and she also knows

I want Ti-grrlz stuff. She buys me a backpack, some books, and a top—all with the Blue Ti-grrlz character.

I'm crushed. How come Mom didn't get me Turquoise? I talk about Turquoise all the time! I know she heard me, but maybe she wasn't really listening. Or maybe the Blue one looked to her like Turquoise.

But I don't tell her I'm disappointed. I know Mom spent a lot of money on these gifts—money she's been nervous about ever since Dad left. Anyhow, I have a brilliant idea: I'll just color the Ti-grrlz stripes with magic marker. Change the blue top to turquoise.

So I do. Except it turns out I'm not as careful at coloring as I thought. Also, the turquoise marker is dry because I use it so much—so the ink runs out halfway through coloring the stripes. And of course now my top looks worse than before.

I decide I can't tell Mom I've ruined her birthday present. I roll up the top into a ball and bury it at the bottom of the laundry hamper.

A few days later Mom does a wash—and when she sees how the marker bled all over the whole load, she's very upset. "What happened to all my work clothes? Mila, do you know why everything's turned blue?"

"I think it's actually turquoise," I say helpfully. "Maybe Hadley threw a crayon in the washing machine."

Hadley is a year and a half old, so we both know that's unlikely.

Mom looks at me and sighs. She's waiting for a better explanation.

I stay quiet. I feel awful about ruining everything—her clothes and mine, especially the Ti-grrlz birthday top. But if I tell her why it happened, I'll have to tell her she got me the wrong present.

She doesn't say a word as she throws everything back in the washing machine. But I'm pretty sure she's figured it out anyway.

LUCKY

Zara was waiting for me outside my homeroom. The first thing I noticed was her tee, which said AFTER A CLAM COMES A STORM. The second thing was that her face didn't have the usual Morning Zara look. She seemed unfoggy, awake.

"Can we talk?" she asked.

I shrugged. "Sure."

"About what happened at lunch yesterday," she said, the words running together. "I wanted to apologize. I should have stuck up for you to the boys—"

"Yeah," I said. "You should have."

"But I was just nervous about the chorus tryout, so I wasn't thinking straight, you know? I just really, really needed to play basketball. And afterward, when I got home, I felt terrible—I couldn't even sleep last night! Can you please forgive me, Mila?"

So here was Zara again: mean, then sorry. Also completely missing the point about the basketball boys.

But how could I not forgive her? Her big dark eyes were wide and begging. She wasn't just saying this stuff—it seemed like she meant it.

"Of course I can," I said.

She threw her arms around me, and we hugged.

Then she pulled away, eying my blue plaid shirt. "Cute top, Mila. I've never seen you wearing it before. Looks comfy."

"Oh, it is."

"Maybe better with leggings, though. Or not. Anyway."

She turned to head for her homeroom, and I thought of something. "Hey, so how did chorus tryouts go yesterday?"

"Crushed it," she called over her shoulder.

The morning zoomed by. Just knowing that things were normal with Zara again made my spine relax a little. Because Zara wasn't First Chair in the Friend Section—but I had to admit she was pretty much the leader.

Also, the basketball boys didn't bother me, not once all morning. Even though in ELA, for our personal memoir project, Mr. Finkelman assigned Dante as my critique partner, which meant he had to read my first two paragraphs.

"Pretty good," he said when he handed me my paper.

And in Spanish we were supposed to have conversations about the airport, using the future tense. Señora Sanchez told me to partner with Leo.

I panicked. And I think he saw the look on my face.

"Nah, it's okay, Mila," he muttered.

Then the two of us did the whole conversation just fine. *Yes, my plane will arrive at two thirty. No, it will not land in Madrid. I will visit Toledo; then I will watch a bullfight.*

Maybe it's over now, I thought.

Maybe today I'm wearing the true lucky shirt.

And then it was lunchtime.

LOCKERS

Just before going to the cafeteria, I went to put away my notebooks. It was another beautiful day, and I wanted to go outside without lugging anything extra.

My locker was in the corner of the first-floor hallway, next to the art studio. Usually the art teacher, Mr. Buono, played music during lunch—classical, mostly, but today was something punk-sounding, probably from when he was a teenager. The song was really loud, and as I was stuffing books into my messy locker, I was trying to make out the words. It sounded like the singer kept asking, "Did you stand by me?"

That was when I felt it.

Someone's hand grabbing my butt.

I spun around.

Tobias.

"Hey, what was that?" I said, barely breathing.

"Nothing." Tobias's eyes were huge. His face and his neck were bright red.

"Don't say *nothing*! I felt your hand just now, Tobias!"

"No, you didn't, Mila. It's probably your imagination."

A sweaty chill came over me. The two of us were alone in the hallway. No one to witness what had happened. And with that music playing so loud, Mr. Buono wouldn't even hear this conversation.

But you don't understand my point of view.
I suppose there's nothing I can do—

Maybe there was a karate move for a situation like this, but I had no idea what it would be.

Just get out of here, I ordered myself. *Now!*

I slammed my locker door and flew down the hall, outdoors to the blacktop.

BABY

The basketball boys were already under the hoop, bouncing the ball to each other. Probably waiting for Tobias.

I raced past them with my head down, past Ms. Wardak, not even caring that I hadn't gone to the lunchroom first, the way we were supposed to. My stomach was in knots; no way could I possibly eat anything.

Where are my friends? How come no one is ever around when I need them?

For the next few minutes (two? three? twenty?) I paced back and forth on the pebble area, hugging myself to try to stop shaking.

Then I saw Tobias slowly coming out to the blacktop. As soon as he joined Leo, Callum, and Dante, I could hear them make whooping noises as they smacked him on the back. While he just stood there, letting himself get smacked.

Are they congratulating him? Like he scored a basket at the buzzer?

So they all know what he just did?

At last Zara, Omi, and Max joined me by the pebbles, laughing about some stupid joke they'd heard in the lunchroom.

Although right away Omi could tell something was up. "Mila, are you okay?"

"Not really," I said. It came out in a gush: what had happened at the lockers with Tobias.

"See?" Zara said. "I *told* you he liked you, Mila."

"No, no!" I shouted desperately. "You're not getting it, Zara—he *doesn't*! And it's not just him! *All* his stupid friends—Dante, Callum, and Leo—they have this *thing* going on. It's like a joke to them, or something, where they make these comments about my body. And try to touch me when no one's watching."

"*Oh*," Zara said. She seemed stunned. "Leo also?"

I nodded. "Remember when I asked you if it was his birthday? It was because he tricked me into hugging him."

"But Mila, why would he do *that*?"

"I don't know! I don't know!"

Omi put her arm around me. I waited for Zara to say something, but she'd gone quiet.

Then Max took a few steps away, his eyes on the untag game. Watching Jared, maybe.

I pulled away from Omi. "Zara? Did you hear what I just—"

"You *know*, Mila," she cut in sharply, "I really don't get why you think all those boys are so obsessed with you. It's a little weird, to be honest. Because you're not the only girl in our grade with boobs."

My mouth dropped open. "I didn't *say* I was! And it's not even about my—"

"So why are you saying they're all so in love with you? Including Leo?"

"Zara, I'm not saying that *at all*! This isn't *about* love, or like; this is about them bothering me!"

"It's bullying," Max said.

That startled me. The way he'd been watching the untag game, I hadn't even realized he'd been listening. And after his disappearance yesterday, I was pretty sure he couldn't do this conversation.

"Mila, I really think you should tell Mr. McCabe," he added.

"Oh, Max, no one's bullying anybody," Zara said, rolling her eyes. "It's called flirting, okay? Don't be such a baby."

The baby thing again.

Max crossed his arms and scowled.

"Well, it sure doesn't feel like flirting to *me*," I said.

"Are you sure?" Zara asked. "How would you know, Mila? Have you ever been flirted with before?"

"Come on, Zara," Omi said softly. "That's not really fair."

Zara ignored her. "Look, Mila, there's got to be a reason why they're picking *you*. Those boys are super awkward and stupid sometimes, but they aren't monsters, right? So maybe if you think about what *you're* doing—"

"I'm not 'doing' anything, Zara!"

"Mila, have you tried talking to them? Telling them how you feel?" Omi asked gently.

"Yes, a bunch of times," I said. "And it totally doesn't work!"

"Well, the last thing you should do is get anyone in trouble, because then they'll just keep teasing, or whatever you want to call it." Zara picked up a pebble and threw it far over everyone's heads, into Not-School. "And you definitely *don't* want to talk to Mr. McCabe, of all people."

I pictured Mr. McCabe's thick pink face and suspicious eyes. The way he coached the basketball boys after school every Monday and Tuesday.

And even though I suspected Zara just didn't want me to report Leo, I couldn't imagine telling all this to Mr. McCabe, anyway.

FRIDAY

On Friday afternoons, the seventh grade invaded town. It was a tradition, I guess: no homework due the next day, and no after-school teams or clubs. So when the weather was nice, instead of taking the bus home, most kids walked a few blocks from school to where the shops were. And they went to Junior Jay's, or the candy store, or the pizza place, or they went to CVS to buy random stuff. But mostly what they did was run up and down the sidewalks and sometimes into the street, where the town cops yelled at them for creating a safety hazard. (I mean, *I* never ran into the street, but I knew plenty of kids who did.)

Today Zara and Omi were planning to go to CVS after school to check out if they had any new nail polish. Max said he had a dentist appointment, which I didn't believe. At lunch, after I'd told him I didn't want to report the boys to Mr. McCabe, he'd gone off to join the untag game, the first time he'd ever done that completely on his own. (Although technically not "on his own"—I noticed he ran right over to Jared.)

Also, when lunch was over, he went to orchestra without saying good-bye to me. So I wondered if maybe he was mad that I'd ignored his advice about telling Mr. McCabe. Or maybe he'd had enough of the whole conversation. Or maybe he just didn't want to hang with us anymore. Or with me.

Wondering all those things made me nervous.

And when Zara and Omi said they were going to CVS for a few minutes, I considered going straight home after school. I didn't have to: Hadley was at her friend Tyler's for a playdate, and on Fridays our neighbor, Mr. Fitzgibbons, walked Delilah with his old dog, Bones. I knew I could take the bus—the basketball boys always did the Friday Thing in town, so I wouldn't have to deal with them on the ride.

But with Max abandoning us the way he was, I could feel my Circle of Friendship shrinking.

So I said I'd go with Zara and Omi, even though:

1) I was still mad at Zara for the stuff she'd said to me at lunch, specifically how I thought the boys were "obsessed" with me. And also about how I should think about what *I* was doing, like any of it was up to me.

2) I had no interest in nail polish.

3) There was a good chance we'd run into the basketball boys.

Which of course we did. It happened right outside Junior Jay's. Omi's abuela had said she'd drive us home at four o'clock, so after fifteen boring minutes in CVS, we were heading back to the school parking lot when someone yelled out, "Hey, it's Mila!"

Behind us there was laughing and hooting. A kind of cheer.

And then someone said, "Hey, where's she going? Wait for us!"

My stomach twisted.

"I need to get out of here," I muttered to Omi and Zara.

Zara grabbed my arm. "No, Mila. You have every right to walk wherever you want. You live here too."

"Yes, I know, but—"

"*No.* You can't keep letting this happen. And if *you* won't stop them, I will."

My throat felt tight. "Zara, please. I just want to deal with it myself."

"Except you're *not* dealing with it, are you."

"Zara, listen to Mila," Omi begged. "She's trying to tell you—"

"I can hear!" Zara exploded. "But we need to stick

up for each other, Omi! If we don't, then we're not really friends, right? Look, Mila, I know you're really upset, so I'm going to end this whole thing for you *right now*. Watch."

She marched about twenty feet over to where Leo, Callum, Dante, Tobias, Luis Garcia, and Daniel Chun were leaning against the wall of Pie in the Sky Pizza. Daniel had a skateboard (had he brought it to school?), and Callum and Luis were eating slices of pizza.

"Hey," Zara said loudly, her hands on her hips. "Guys! I want to tell you something, so you'd better listen. Mila is getting sick of all that obnoxious stuff you're doing. And I am too. So if you don't want to deal with *me*, you'd better cut it out. Okay?"

Crap. The boys stared at her. Dante whispered something to Tobias, who smiled.

"What stuff?" Leo asked. He made an innocent face.

"Don't pretend you don't know," Zara said. All of a sudden, she did something I wasn't expecting. She actually *smiled* at him. "Because you know, Leo, if you keep bothering Mila, I'll start to get jealous."

What?

WHAT?

Omi's eyes met mine. Just for a second, then looked away.

"Aww, come on, Zara, we didn't mean anything," Leo protested.

"Well, you better stop anyway," Zara said. She did a small barky laugh.

But now Leo was looking past her and waving at me, his whole arm in a sweeping motion, like he was saying farewell to a ship. "Hey Mila, don't be mad, we didn't mean anything!"

"Yeah, right," I snarled.

Luis and Daniel were laughing.

Callum didn't say a word. He just stood there, calmly eating a slice of pizza.

"Well, okay, then," Zara said. I couldn't tell if she felt weird about Leo not teasing her back, or if she'd even noticed. "So now you've all heard me, okay? Leave Mila alone, especially *you*, Tobias. And you guys better not make me tell you again."

She marched back over to Omi and me.

"Mission accomplished," she said.

HELP

I didn't know if Zara expected a thank-you from me or a compliment. Probably both.

"See, Mila?" she said as we headed back to the school parking lot to meet Omi's abuela. "That wasn't so hard, was it? All you need to do is—"

I couldn't bear to listen. "Zara, I don't know what you thought you were doing, but you didn't solve *anything* just now. At *all*."

She turned to me, shocked. "What do you mean?"

"You made it all about you, how great *you* are. What a good friend. And you made *me* look like a helpless baby."

"What? Mila, that's so unfair! I thought you were mad at me yesterday for *not* sticking up for you. I even felt bad about it afterward! And so now when I *do*—"

"All you *really* care about is Leo," I blurted.

Zara's mouth fell open. "Excuse me?"

"You were so flirting with him just now! And in case it isn't obvious, Zara, I don't *want* his stupid attention! Or *any* of theirs. And yes, I *did* want you to stick up for me yesterday. But not like *that*."

She snorted. "Well, sorry for my *technique*."

"Mila, Zara was just trying to be a good friend," Omi said. Her face looked smaller, like a dried-up flower.

"Then she should have listened to me," I snapped. I was so mad by now that my knees were shaking. "And *if* she was sticking up for me, she shouldn't be flirting with her crush!"

Zara stopped walking. She crossed her arms. "Mila," she said too loudly. "Can I ask you something? Do you think it's possible that Leo was right—the boys were just fooling around? And maybe *you* were being a little too sensitive?"

"No," I said. "That's not possible."

"Because it feels like you're just criticizing *everyone!* Everything everyone does is wrong with you lately!"

"All right, I think that's slightly exaggerating," Omi said. Her lips were trembling; she looked like she might start crying. Because I knew she hated fights worse than anything.

Zara kept her fierce dark eyes on me. "And seriously, Mila, if that's the kind of friend you think I am, why did I even bother?"

"I don't know, Zara," I said. "Why did you?"

Zara opened her mouth to answer. Then I guess she decided against it, because she spun around and headed back to CVS.

Omi's abuela picked us up at four o'clock on the dot. She was that kind of organized.

And the whole ride to my house, Omi barely said a word. Her abuela chatted about how they were having their roof repaired, what she was making for supper, and some dentist appointment she needed to reschedule, and Omi just kept saying, "Sí, Abuelita," and "Okay." It reminded me of the conversations I had with Hadley. *Huh. Uh-huh.*

Finally, when we pulled up to my driveway, Omi put her arm around my shoulders. "Zara messed up, I know. She should have listened better, she shouldn't have acted that way with Leo, and she always blows up too fast. But please don't be angry with her, okay?"

"Why not?" I asked. "Why shouldn't I be?"

"Because I think she was only trying to help," Omi said. "And to be honest, Mila, right now you really need all the friends you have."

PHONE

When I opened the door, I expected I'd have the house to myself. Except for Delilah, if she was back from her walk with Mr. Fitzgibbons and Bones.

Instead I heard Mom's voice coming from the living room. She was home too early. The way she was talking, I could tell she was on her phone. And upset.

"No, I mean it.

"Well, but I'm tired of waiting.

"When?

"Oh, but you're always busy!

"You know what? I'm sick of feeling helpless, I really am. I know you've moved on, I totally get that, but these are still your kids! And if I need to call a lawyer—

"Then it's up to you, isn't it. I don't know what else—

"No, I—

"No, this conversation is over.

"That's all I have to say. I'm hanging up now.

"Good-bye, Kevin."

I stood there, frozen.

She'd been talking to Dad.

DON'T

"Hey, I'm home," I sang out. "Delilah, are you here?"

No barking or scampering to greet me. As I expected.

I walked into the living room. "Delilah, are you—oh, hi, Mom. Why are you home so early?"

Mom looked at me, blinking. Her eyes and nose were pink and her face was blotchy. She was still wearing her worky clothes and black pumps. "Oh, hi, sweetheart. I didn't hear you come in. You went to town just now with your friends, and Omi's grandma drove you back?"

I nodded. She hadn't answered my question.

"And did you have a nice time?" she asked.

I couldn't possibly tell her. Not when she looked like a crumpled tissue.

"Yeah, it was great," I said. "The whole school was there, practically. Are you feeling okay?"

"Actually, my stomach was a little upset. So I thought maybe I'd work from home this afternoon."

But you weren't working; you were on the phone with Dad. "You want me to make you some tea?" I asked.

"Oh yes—chamomile would be great. Thank you, sweetheart!"

I put down my backpack and went into the kitchen to fill the teakettle. After it was heating on the stove for a minute, I could hear Mom's phone ring, and her answering, but I couldn't make out the words. Just that she was speaking very fast, but quietly, as if she didn't want me to hear.

I brought out the tea in a mug that used to say ADOPT, DON'T SHOP. We got it from Delilah's shelter. By now most of the letters had rubbed off, so what it said was DO, DON'T.

"Here's your tea, Mom," I said in a cheery voice.

"Just exactly what I needed. Thank you." Mom gave me a shaky smile. "Nice to have a quiet minute with you before Delilah gets back. And Hadley."

It is?

I took a breath. "Mom, is everything okay? I mean at work."

Mom put the mug on the small table next to the sofa. "Why are you asking?"

"I don't know, just wondering. You keep saying your boss is mean. And yesterday you were crying. But then at Junior Jay's you told us you were getting a raise—"

"No, sweetheart, I said maybe." She closed her eyes for just a second. "And today I found out that's not going to happen. I'm very sorry."

"Oh." Then I couldn't stop myself. "And that's why you were on the phone to Dad just now? To ask him for more money?"

Mom's face puckered. I'd never told her I knew Dad wasn't sending us checks the way he was supposed to. In fact, we barely talked about Dad at all.

"You overheard my phone conversation?" she asked softly.

"Yeah, when I came home. I didn't mean to; I couldn't help it. I'm sorry."

"Well, I'm sorry you heard it, sweetheart; it was between Dad and me, and I'd rather not discuss it. But you know it has nothing to do with how Dad feels about you girls. He still loves you and Hadley very much."

"Okay," I said.

Like I believed what Mom was saying. Like we didn't both know the truth.

She sighed. "Anyway, Mila, I'm dealing with it, and we'll be fine. So you don't need to worry about anything, okay? Especially money. And please don't mention it to Hadley."

"What would I mention?"

"Just, you know. Don't."

We looked at each other.

Then Mom remembered her tea and took a long sip.

"DING DONG!" Mr. Fitzgibbons yelled. Because he walked Delilah on Fridays, he had a key to our house, but he never liked to use it if he thought someone might be home. And he was old and very polite; he never came inside, he said, because he didn't want his dog, Bones, to "muddy up the floors," even though Delilah's paws were just as dirty. So he always just stood there yelling "DING DONG" until we came to the front door.

Mom jumped off the sofa, and the two of us went to greet Delilah and thank Mr. Fitzgibbons.

"Delilah is no trouble, no trouble at all," he kept saying, waving away the twenty-dollar bill Mom offered. Whenever Mom saw Mr. Fitzgibbons, she tried to pay him, but he always refused.

Then he started chatting about some new organic dog food he was feeding Bones.

"I'll give you a sample to try on Delilah," he said.

"That's sweet, but you really don't have to," Mom said.

"I insist," Mr. Fitzgibbons said. "My treat. See you next week, Delilah!"

Mom closed the door behind Mr. Fitzgibbons and looked at me with wettish eyes.

"Always remember that there are true gentlemen in the world," she said.

BROCHURE

On Saturday morning Hadley reminded Mom that we were supposed to go to Old Navy. And I reminded Hadley that Mom had said she needed to go to work instead.

"Actually, girls, I'm not going into work," Mom announced. "And let's hold off shopping another week, okay?"

"Aww!" Hadley pouted. "Mommy, you promised. You said I could get purple leggings, and a pink down vest—"

"And I haven't forgotten, Had. I'm just thinking this isn't the best time to be spending money."

I glanced at Mom, who was biting her thumbnail. What did she mean by "isn't the best time"? Was she getting fired? Maybe she should go into the office after all.

"But I have a great idea instead," Mom added brightly.

"How about if we three go to E Motions this afternoon? They have a whole bunch of weekend classes—"

Hadley's eyes popped. "YAY! I wanna do tap-dancing and hip-hop and summer salts—"

She said it with a little pause between "summer" and "salts"—like they were different from "winter salts."

"It's somersaults, not *summer salts*," I said, rolling my eyes. "And who knows if they even have a class about that, Hadley."

"Oh, I bet they offer some sort of gymnastics," Mom said. "Let's check the brochure."

She left the table and returned with a small blue booklet that looked like a takeout menu.

"All the classes look so great!" Mom exclaimed with too much enthusiasm. "Okay, Had, how about this one? 'Mat-tastic! Learn the basics of tumbling—'"

"Is tumbling summer salts?" Hadley asked.

"*Somersaults*, and yes," I said.

"That one!" Hadley yelled, jumping. "Okay? Mommy? Okay?"

Mom laughed. "Sure, baby. What about you, Mila?"

She pushed the brochure across the table so I could see it. All her nails looked raw and chewed, not just her thumb. And that surprised me, because mom nails weren't supposed to look like that.

"Is there something here you'd like to do, sweetheart?"

she asked me. "Remember, it's still the trial period, so we get to take all their classes for free."

But only for two weeks, so what was the point? You couldn't learn anything much in two weeks.

I looked at my little sister, who was still jumping, and Mom, trying hard to act cheerful. Whatever was going on with her at work, she didn't want us to know about it, which made it seem worse. She also seemed like she needed to burn some energy, to quote Zara.

And of course, quoting Zara made me think about everything that had happened at school—and after school—with my friends. The weirdness with Tobias. Zara scolding the boys in town. Our fight afterward. How Max had wandered off at lunch, and Omi had told me I needed friends.

But what good are friends when they don't listen?

Or, when they do listen, don't understand?

I need to take care of myself.

By myself.

And suddenly I had an answer. Maybe not a solution, but an answer to Mom's question.

"Karate," I said.

STRETCH

Ms. Brennan, so glad to see you again." Ms. Platt was smiling. Also waiting for something, apparently.

But what? My shoes were already off.

"Um, hi," I said. "I'm only here for the trial membership, so that's why I don't have a uniform."

"You mean a gi."

"Right, a gi. Or a belt."

"That's okay," Ms. Platt said. Her eyes twinkled. And she still didn't move.

Behind her, Samira caught my eye. *Bow,* she mouthed. She made a bowing motion.

Oh, right.

I bowed at Ms. Platt, who bowed back.

"Ms. Brennan, we always start class with some stretches,"

she said. "I'm going to pair you with Ms. Spurlock; she'll demonstrate for you on the mat."

My heart sank. I hadn't even been here for a minute, and already I was supposed to follow Ms. Spurlock—Samira—who was apparently teacher's pet here, too. Or sensei's pet, or whatever we were supposed to call it.

But right away, Samira explained she'd been studying karate at a different dojo for the past two years, so she really did know what to do. She showed me a bunch of stretches—sitting, kneeling, standing—that she said warmed up hamstrings, side muscles, and knees. And she didn't act all *look how great I am* about it; it was more like she cared that I learn the right way.

"Try not to jerk or bounce, Ms. Brennan," she told me. "Be gentle and slow."

Okay, I thought. *But I'm not here for gentle and slow. And are you really going to call me Ms. Brennan? Because seriously.*

A few more kids arrived—an Asian-American girl who looked about eight, a redheaded girl around my age, a tiny dark-skinned boy with a chirpy voice, a scary-pale teen girl with a nose ring.

"All jewelry off, Ms. Nathan," Ms. Platt told her. Her voice was friendly, but stern.

"Oh, come on," the girl begged. "It won't be an issue, Ms. Platt, I promise."

"Ms. Nathan, you know the rules of the dojo. Let's not waste time. Remove the jewelry, and then I'd like to see Mr. Chowdhury and Ms. Spurlock lead the first three shobus. Ms. Spurlock and Mr. Chowdhury, get your distance, please."

The other kids lined up on the mat, so I did too. And we watched Samira and the chirpy-voiced boy do some moves, over and over, while Ms. Platt narrated. ("Step back, arms in, Ms. Spurlock, remember to lead with the top two knuckles; now parry-block, Mr. Chowdhury, very nice, now reverse.")

Then Ms. Platt lifted her arms. "Now, the rest of us, let's develop some muscle memory. Hajime."

The other kids started doing the moves, and by now, after all those repetitions, I could do them too. Well, pretty much. Ms. Platt made herself my partner, the whole time saying things like "Bend the elbow forty-five degrees, straighten that leg, bigger step." But I didn't feel embarrassed or helpless or singled out. Just like when Samira had paired with me for the stretches, Ms. Platt seemed to be cheering me on, happy when I finally did a straightforward punch "clean and sharp."

After that we all practiced front kicks and side-blade kicks while Ms. Platt counted in Japanese. We did the kicks over and over, until my thigh muscles ached and the soles of my feet tingled.

• • •

I got sweaty. I even did a kiai so loud that Ms. Nathan, the no-nose-ring girl, high-fived me. Afterward Samira came over. "So? Isn't karate great?"

"Yes," I said. "It's really fun."

"And Mila, I think it's *such* a good idea that you're taking it," she murmured. "Because of all that stuff with the boys at school."

I nodded. "Yeah. That was pretty much the idea."

But I couldn't help thinking:

What does any of today—
the bowing, the counting in Japanese,
even the moves on the mat
which kind of look like dance steps—
have to do with
the laughing on the blacktop
the comments
the contact on the bus
at the lockers
in the band room?

BUSINESS

"**M**ila, wake up."

I didn't want to; I was in the middle of a dream. Not a fun dream—I was racing around a complicated train station, lost and late for something—but it felt too real to turn off the switch.

"Mmf," I said. "Why?"

Mom gently shook my shoulder. "I need to talk to you, honey," she said.

I sat up. My mouth was sour and pasty, like I'd swallowed a slug. "What time is it?"

"Eight thirty."

"Aren't I late for school?"

"No, honey, it's Sunday. But I'm going into work—"

"Wait, what?" My brain swirled. "I thought you said—"

"Yes, but now my boss says I need to go in. For a special meeting."

"On a Sunday?" I rubbed my crusty eyes. She wasn't even wearing her worky clothes. "Mom, that's crazy. And not fair."

"I know." She paused. "I told Mr. Fitzgibbons to check if you needed anything, and Molly Ames says she'll stop by for Hadley—"

I groaned. "*Please* not her. I'll just watch Hadley myself."

"Well, Molly's already agreed to come, and she's bringing Cherish. Unless I'm back before lunch, which could very well happen. I don't know."

Slowly the whole thing was coming into focus. "Mom, why would you be back before lunch? I mean, if you're going all the way to the office—"

"Because it's possible I'm getting fired, sweetheart," Mom said quietly. "You know, my boss really has it in for me these days."

"But how come? You never talk about it."

She sighed.

"Mom, I'm not a baby," I said.

She reached over to smooth my bed head. "I know you aren't, sweetheart. All right, really fast, because I need to leave: I noticed some figures in the financials that weren't adding up, so I reported it to my boss's boss. And of course when *my* boss found out, he got furious. At me." She did a small sideways smile that wasn't a smile at all. "But let's not worry about stuff before it happens. Okay?"

"Okay," I told her.

But by now I was sure of one thing: the way she kept telling me *not* to worry, there was definitely something to worry about.

JACKET

About an hour later the doorbell rang. It was Mrs. Ames and Cherish, who was holding a floppy yellow terry-cloth bunny in her right hand and sucking her left thumb. Mrs. Ames was wearing bright red lipstick and a black motorcycle jacket with too many zippers.

"Good morning, Mila!" Mrs. Ames exclaimed. "Is Hadley ready?"

"For what?" I asked. It definitely didn't come out as polite as I meant it, and for a second I thought she'd threaten to report me to Mr. McCabe.

But she did her too-big smile. "It's so great out—I thought we'd take a walk over to the park and bring Delilah. And of course you're welcome to join us, Mila."

"No thank you," I said. "I've got homework."

"Another *project*?" Mrs. Ames actually winked at me.

I pretended not to notice. "Hadley!" I yelled.

My little sister shuffled to the door. She was all dressed to go, except she was wearing faded pink pj bottoms.

"Hadley, you can't go out like that," I said.

"Oh, sure she can," Mrs. Ames said in a drippy voice. "It's totally fine, honey."

"Well, Mom likes us to dress *normally*," I said, glancing at the motorcycle jacket. "Hadley, don't you have any leggings—"

"No!" Hadley shouted. "Mommy said she'd take us shopping to *buy* some. And she isn't *here*."

Hadley's lower lip was pouting, and the way her voice wobbled, I thought she might have a meltdown.

So did Mrs. Ames, I guess, because she grabbed Hadley's hand. "Well, Mommy had some important business to take care of this morning, muffin. I'm sure she'll take you shopping as soon as she possibly can. Where's Delilah?"

"I'll go get her," I muttered.

I went to the living room. Delilah was sleeping on our old sofa, the way she did most of the time these days. I threw my arms around her, inhaling her burned-toast sort of smell. Then I poked her belly to wake her up. She snuffled, stretched her back legs, and kept on sleeping.

And the whole time I was poking our old dog awake, I was thinking how lucky she was, to be dreaming doggy dreams for a few extra seconds before she had to get up and face the non-sofa world.

OMI

A little while after Mrs. Ames left with Hadley and Delilah, two things happened.

The first was that Omi showed up—without calling or even texting first. Apparently she was coming straight from church, so she was dressed in a way I'd never seen before: a pale blue dress with a white cardigan, ballet flats, her hair in a neat little bun, with barrettes. She looked like a second grader, but pretty.

"Mila, can I talk to you?" she asked at the door. She seemed out of breath, even though her abuelo's car was in our driveway, so she couldn't have walked over. "I mean, in private? Now?"

"Actually, yeah," I said. "Nobody's home. Not even Delilah."

"I just need to tell my abuelo." Omi ran over to the car, said something in Spanish through the open window, then came running back. "I can only stay ten minutes. We're on our way to Tía Rosario's house."

"Does your grandpa want to come in? I can make some tea—"

"He says he'll wait in the car."

The way Omi's face looked—pinched and pale, the opposite of her regular expression—made me not ask questions. I led her into our tiny kitchen.

"We can talk here," I said, suddenly embarrassed about how messy the counter looked and how the dishes were piled up in the sink. Mom hadn't even cleaned up breakfast before she left for work, which was extremely weird for her. "Or we could go in my bedroom," I added. "Or the living room, but it smells like dog—"

"Here is fine. Mila, I have to tell you something. It's really bad."

My stomach tightened. "Okay."

"After church just now, Hunter came over to me. And he showed me something on his phone."

"Wait," I said. "Hunter Schultz? Max's enemy?"

"Yeah, but he's not like that anymore. He's different now."

"Okaaay," I said doubtfully.

Omi twisted her hands. "So anyway, what he showed

151

me was this sort of game the boys are playing. Like a score-card."

"Uh-huh." My mouth dried up. I felt cold.

"And Mila, it was about *you*. The points were for saying things to you, touching your body, your clothes—" Omi's hand flew to her mouth, and she started crying. "I'm so sorry."

"For what?" I said. "You didn't do anything."

I grabbed a paper towel and handed it to her. Part of me was in shock. Another part of me wasn't surprised at all. The way the basketball boys had cheered Tobias after the thing at my locker—it really *had* seemed like a game. A sport.

"So can I see this scorecard?" I asked.

Omi dried her eyes as she shook her head. "No. I mean, I asked Hunter to send it to me, but he wouldn't. He said he didn't want to get anyone in trouble."

"Wow, what a nice friend."

"Well, but it *was* nice to show it to me, wasn't it? He didn't have to."

"I guess." I swallowed hard. It felt like there were pebbles in my throat. "So does everyone else know about this?"

"I'm not sure. But *I'm* not telling anyone. Not even Zara, if you don't want me to."

Zara? But I couldn't think about her right then.

And now my mind was racing. What exactly was I supposed to do with this information? Even if I wanted to report it to Mr. McCabe, I didn't have any evidence. The boys could just deny this game even existed. And Hunter wouldn't be any sort of witness, if he refused to send the game to Omi.

As for Omi, she was a great friend, maybe my only true friend left. But I couldn't imagine her accusing anyone. And risking Zara's anger—not to mention taking on all those boys.

"Mila, I've been thinking about this a lot," Omi was saying, "and from now on you really shouldn't be by yourself at school, okay? Try to walk next to other people, don't go to the lockers all alone, always have a witness—"

"Omi, that's impossible!"

"Probably, but you need to *try*." She threw her arms around me in a hug. "And maybe soon it'll stop, anyway."

"Why would it?" I asked bitterly.

"Because it can't just keep happening," Omi said.

FINE

The second thing that morning:

An hour later, at eleven forty-five, Mom burst through the front door, her arms full of groceries.

"Where's Hadley?" she asked.

"At the park with Mrs. Ames. And Cherish. And Delilah."

She started throwing things into the fridge—and out of it. I mean literally *throwing*, not carefully placing, the way she usually did.

"Mom, are you okay?" I asked as she tossed an old head of romaine lettuce across the kitchen, missing the trash can by a few feet.

"I am *absolutely fine*," she declared. "And I have big news. Guess what, Mila—I quit my job!"

I stared. "You did? I mean, just now when you went to the office?"

"Yes! And we'll be *fine*, so don't worry. Will you please hand me that sponge?"

I gave it to her. "That boss was a jerk to you, anyway, Mom. Right?"

"Yes, he was! And I deserve better. This *whole family* deserves better!"

She started scrubbing the counter, the whole time talking about how great she felt, how positive this was, how she was absolutely going to find another job right away, with a better boss who was a decent, honest person. And for more money, too, probably.

A few minutes later Mrs. Ames, Hadley, Cherish, and Delilah walked in, and Mom repeated the whole speech. Even louder the second time.

"Mommy?" Hadley said when Mom finally took a breath. "Does this mean we can go to Old Navy today? And I can get purple leggings?"

Mom threw her head back and laughed, as if this were the funniest, cutest thing any kid had ever said. "Of course it does, baby. And afterward we'll go to E Motions, and then out to dinner at Junior Jay's!"

GAME

Mom insisted on buying lots of clothes at Old Navy, not just for Hadley, but also for me. And even though I was definitely freaked about Mom quitting her job, which meant we'd have even less money than usual, I was also really glad for a few new things—three loose-fitting cotton sweaters in dark purple, navy, and black. Two pairs of jeans that fit without tugging. So I didn't resist, although when we were back in the car and Mom started complaining about the price of gasoline, I wondered if maybe I should have.

We got to E Motions at three forty-five. Mom had checked the Sunday schedule on her phone, so we knew there was an exercise class she could do at four, and Hadley could try something called "jazz dance" at four fifteen.

As for me, I didn't feel like moving much anyway. I was still sort of in a daze. Not only about the Mom-quitting-her-job-and-would-we-starve thing. Also about the boys-playing-a-game-about-me thing. Even more about that one, to be honest.

And the more I thought about it, the angrier I felt.

I'm a game?

You score points by bumping into me?

Maybe the hug is five points.

And the butt grab is twenty-five.

What are the comments worth?

Maybe a point if I don't respond.

Or a point if I do.

And also:

Who else knows about this stupid game?

If Hunter knows, he can't be the only one.

Maybe all his friends know.

Maybe the whole seventh grade.

Even—

For example,

Liana Brock, who makes her face go blank—

the girls.

BREAKFAST

Monday morning was weird. Usually Mom spent all of breakfast urging us to hurry up, eat our breakfast, get out the door. But today she was sort of drowsy, still in her pj's and robe, even though Hadley needed to get to her bus stop and afterward I needed her to drive me to school.

"So what are you going to do today?" I asked Mom as I drowned some Hunny Flakes with two-percent milk.

"Oh, I don't know," she said, yawning. "Start the job search, I suppose."

Shouldn't you be more awake for that? And a little more . . . dressed?

"Mommy, you should get some purple leggings," Hadley declared. "Then we'll be twins."

Mom smiled. "That would be fun. Hey, speaking of

purple leggings: After school today, who wants to go to E Motions?"

"Meeee!" yelled Hadley.

"Mila, what about you?"

I shrugged. "Sure. But Mom, shouldn't you—"

Mom raised her eyebrows. "Shouldn't I what?"

Be looking for a job. Not wasting time on some exercise class.

I guess Mom could tell what I was thinking because she said, "In case you're wondering, Mila, I'll be making a bunch of calls this morning. I have a few leads I'm feeling hopeful about. And going to E Motions is great for stress. Not that I'm feeling any in particular; I just mean in general."

"Okay," I said.

She drank some coffee. "So don't be late after school. No 'projects,' okay?"

I didn't answer. But I peeked at Hadley, who was eating her Oaties one by one, with her fingers. Had she told Mom I'd been late the other day, even though she'd promised to keep it a secret? Or was it Mrs. Ames?

I had a strong feeling it was Mrs. Ames.

But either way, the thought that I'd have to take the bus home today—and maybe every day, until Mom got another job—made my stomach knot.

APOLOGY

"Hey, Mila, nice top," Zara said. She'd been waiting for me outside my homeroom, apparently. Was this going to be the apology part of the Zara Cycle? After the mean part?

Although, wait—*had* there been a mean part?

I mentally scrolled back to our fight on Friday. Zara had said and done a bunch of things that made me furious, but to be honest, I couldn't remember any *actual meanness*.

I blinked at her tee, which said FEEL ENJOY! Underneath the words was a smiling marshmallow with arms and legs.

"Thanks," I said. "Mom took us shopping yesterday."

"Well, purple's a good color on you. Anyway."

Zara smiled uncertainly. Suddenly I realized she was waiting for *me* to apologize, which was crazy, really. Because I knew I hadn't done anything wrong—and even if Zara hadn't acted mean to me, she'd ignored my feelings about confronting the boys, she'd flirted with Leo (which I still couldn't believe), and, who knows, possibly she'd made everything even worse.

But I had to admit Omi was right: I needed my friends. Especially now that the boys were sharing that scorecard.

"Sorry about Friday," I blurted. "I shouldn't have said that stuff to you. I know you were only trying to stick up for me."

"Aww, Mila, you were just upset," Zara said. "It's okay." She threw her arms around me and squeezed.

I waited for her to say, *And I'm sorry too.* But she never did.

And that was how I knew I couldn't tell her about the scorecard.

STAND

I knew Omi's advice to me—always keep surrounded, always have witnesses—made sense, but of course no way could I actually follow it. Not knowing who knew about the scorecard, who had seen the other stuff going on, who knew but was pretending not to—I couldn't trust my classmates to protect me. Plus, forcing myself to constantly stand next to people, walk in a group, felt kind of like hiding. And the idea that I needed to hide myself made me feel like I'd done something wrong. Which I definitely hadn't.

So except for lunch, I basically kept to myself. Quiet, careful, alert.

Nothing bad happened.

Until band.

. . .

When I got to the band room, Leo was in my seat, talking to Callum and Dante.

"Excuse me," I said.

They ignored me. I said it again.

Leo looked up. His hair was falling over his eyes in a way Zara probably liked. "Yeah?"

"You know exactly, Leo," I said. "You're in my chair. And class is about to start, so I need to set up my stand and everything, okay?"

Leo murmured something to Callum and Dante, who both laughed. Then he walked off to the saxophone section, and Dante took his chair in the row behind us.

"Yeah, Mila, about the music stand," Callum said. "We need to share it today. I left my music home, so I'm going to look on with you."

Not *Can I*. Or *Would it be okay if*. Or *Please*.

"Actually, I don't think that's going to work," I said through my teeth.

He seemed surprised. "Why not?"

"Because, Callum, I don't *want* to share with you."

His eyes widened. "Really? Well, too bad, Mila. Because I'm the leader of this section, and we're practicing my solo today. And Ms. Fender won't be happy if you mess me up."

"And neither will the rest of the band," Dante said from behind me.

I could feel my face getting hot, all the way to my scalp. I wanted to yell, but I didn't want anyone else to hear this conversation. So I angry-whispered, "Oh, and if I *do* share my stand, how much is that worth to you, Callum? A point? Two points?"

"What are you talking about?" Callum asked. He said this in his normal voice, so everyone could hear. Which made me even madder.

"Don't pretend like you don't know," I muttered. "You guys have this stupid scorecard. I know all about it, okay?"

Callum actually laughed. *Laughed.*

"Come on," he said. "It doesn't mean anything, Mila. It's just a game."

That was when Ms. Fender hurried across the room. "Sorry for the delay. Let's take 'Pirate Medley' from the second section all the way to the end of the tenth measure. Samira, I want to hear that B-flat nice and round this time. Trombones, keep a steady beat. Callum, when it's your solo, please stand. Ready, band? I want to see perfect posture, open chests. A *one* and a *two*—"

I pressed my dry lips on the mouthpiece. But my chest felt tight, and it was hard to breathe.

It doesn't mean anything. It's just a game.

And when Callum stood to play his first note—C—he

sounded so loud it made my bones vibrate.

It was like my whole body was being invaded.

So, not thinking *This is what I'm going to do, and this is what will happen next,* I front-kicked the music stand, and "Pirate Medley" went flying.

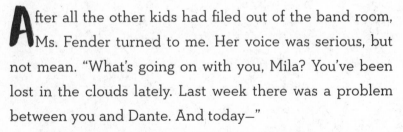

WELL

After all the other kids had filed out of the band room, Ms. Fender turned to me. Her voice was serious, but not mean. "What's going on with you, Mila? You've been lost in the clouds lately. Last week there was a problem between you and Dante. And today—"

"I'm so sorry!" I blurted. "My foot slipped."

"No, Mila, it didn't. I was watching. You kicked that music stand on purpose."

I felt like I'd fallen down a well. *Thud.*

"I promise it won't happen again," I said in a strangled-sounding voice.

Then she looked at me the way Mom did, as if she were searching for something specific. A hidden clue.

"Mila, may I ask you something?" she said gently. Not

using a teacher voice at all. "Is everything okay? I mean at home."

I was so shocked by this question all I could do was nod.

"Because I know sometimes when kids are dealing with family problems, like illness or divorce, they keep it to themselves." Her gray eyes were big and soft. "But eventually it spills out. Usually at school."

"My family is fine. We're all doing great, actually."

Although, to be honest, I'm only guessing about Dad. But Mom is doing okay, for a jobless person.

"And you're getting along with all your friends?"

"Yeah. Pretty much."

If you don't count all the fights with Zara. And the fact that Max is sort of pulling away.

Ms. Fender sighed. She rubbed her forehead with long, graceful fingers. "Well, I'm very sorry to do this, Mila, but since I've already had to speak to you about your behavior once, now I'm changing your position."

Changing my position?

That meant sticking me in the back row with all the kids who didn't take lessons over the summer, never practiced at home, didn't come early for extra rehearsal. And probably never even heard the blue-sky sound on their trumpets.

"Oh no, you don't need to do that!" I begged. "Please!"

"Unfortunately, I think I do." Ms. Fender was upset, but

knowing that wasn't making me feel any better. "You know, I put you next to Callum because right now he's our strongest trumpet player. But I've always thought you had the potential to be first chair one day. Unless I'm wrong about you. Have I been wrong about you, Mila?"

She searched my face again, looking for clues. But the shame burning my throat hurt too much to answer.

DIFFERENT

The whole rest of school, my stomach was squirmy about what Ms. Fender had said to me, and also about taking the bus home. But at 2:35, when the bell rang for dismissal, I remembered one good thing: today was Monday, which meant the boys would be staying for basketball practice with Mr. McCabe. So that meant I wouldn't have to deal with them on the bus ride home. Woohoo.

I took a seat near the window, breathing normally for the first time all afternoon.

Samira and Annabel took the seat in front of me. I thought they'd ignore me, the way they usually did. But not today.

"Mila, what happened in band today?" Annabel asked. "Why'd you kick Callum's stand like that?"

"It wasn't *his* stand; it was mine," I said. "And lately he's been driving me crazy."

"Yeah, I know what you mean. He thinks he's the star. I mean, he's a good trumpet player, but." She rolled her eyes.

"Well, anyhow, Mila, your kick was clean and sharp." Samira grinned at me. "Right on target."

"Thank you." I grinned back.

"So are you coming to karate today?"

"I guess."

"Why aren't you sure?"

"It's complicated. Stuff with my mom."

She nodded. Everyone had *stuff with their mom.* "But you do like karate, right? You told me you did."

"Yeah, it's fun. But." I shrugged.

"But what?"

"I don't know what it's *for*, exactly."

"Seriously?" Samira's eyes flashed behind her glasses. "Karate makes you stronger. And also feel better."

"I guess."

Her eyes snapped. "Mila, you've been there *twice*. You can't expect to feel different after just two classes!"

I knew she was right: two classes weren't anything. And two weeks wouldn't be much better.

But do I want to feel different?

From what?

Myself?

INTRO

If Mom had made any progress with the job search, she didn't say so when I walked in the door. At least she didn't seem sleepy anymore, or even upset; she just seemed twitchy, like she couldn't wait for Hadley and me to get home from school, so we could go to E Motions and do sit-ups, or stretches, or whatever it was she did there.

"Don't you want to change your clothes, girls?" she asked us as she was tying her sneakers. "Maybe a good idea not to get your new stuff all sweaty."

"No, Mommy, I *promise* I won't get sweaty," Hadley begged.

"Had, you're missing the whole point of exercising," I said.

But we couldn't convince her, and Mom's Jazzercise class started in twelve minutes, so I just threw on a faded tee and some old yoga pants that tugged across my hips, and the three of us got in the car and drove over.

"Hey there, Mila and Hadley," Erica greeted us in the reception area, flashing her white smile. "This must be your mom?" She held out her hand for Mom to shake.

Mom laughed into her chin. It was funny to see her act shy. "Call me Amy," Mom told her.

"Well, Amy, we're so pleased to welcome your whole family to our club! And as soon as you're all settled on classes, we'll do the paperwork and settle your membership fees. I think your free intro offer runs out pretty soon?"

Erica did the same dorky little move that I'd thought was her dance move. Maybe it was how she communicated "e motions" in general.

Mom blinked. "Yes, that's right. But we still have about a week left, I think."

"Well, enjoy your free classes! And when you're ready to sign up, come find me. I'm always around here somewhere; I used to have an office manager, but now it's all just me!"

"Okay, yes, I absolutely will," Mom said. "Thanks."

I peeked at her. Was Mom serious about signing up? She seemed to be, but that made no sense. Not if she didn't even have a job.

I used to be able to tell when she was fibbing, but lately I wasn't so sure.

SURPRISE

In the karate room Samira was talking to Ms. Platt in the far corner, over by the black pads we used for kicking practice. I didn't think anything about it until Ms. Platt made an announcement at the start of class.

"Today I thought we'd change things up a bit," she said. "Instead of regular karate class, we're going to practice some simple strategies for self-defense. Because let's be real: outside this dojo, if you're threatened with attack, you won't be on a mat, wearing a gi, with me right there to coach you."

Samira was sitting a few feet away, next to Destiny Nathan, the no-nose-ring girl. Our eyes met, and right away I knew. Samira had told Ms. Platt about the basketball boys.

The funny thing was, I didn't feel embarrassed. Or even mad at her, really.

"Everybody, please rise," Ms. Platt said. "No Japanese today, and we'll all use first names. Destiny, let's pretend you're walking down your street, minding your own business, when all of a sudden someone leans out of a car and makes a nasty comment about your outfit. How do you react?"

Destiny snorted. "Excuse me, moron, but who asked for your stupid opinion about my clothes? First of all, I *know* my outfit is cool, because I wouldn't wear it if it wasn't, okay? And second of all, I'm sorry, dude, but how can you even see anything from your car?"

"Okay, stop," Ms. Platt said, smiling a little. "Too many words, Destiny. Don't ever say 'excuse me' or 'sorry,' and don't end sentences with questions. First rule of self-defense is: Don't ask your attacker for validation. Never apologize for sticking up for yourself. Let's try it again. Samira, pretend you fail your math test, and some kid in your class calls you stupid."

"Well, I'm not," Samira said loudly. "And I'll prove it by not even having this conversation." She crossed her arms over her chest.

"Nice," Ms. Platt said. "I like the way you refused to engage. But don't cross your arms, Samira; that communicates vulnerability. Aim for a confident, relaxed stance, good posture, neutral expression on your face, hands open and in front of you. *Or hands on your hips; that looks more confrontational, which may be what you want, depending on the circumstances.* Also, don't *say* you're not having the conversation; just don't have it. The shorter the verbal response, the better."

"Can we kiai?" Jacob asked.

"No, Jacob," Destiny said. "Not outside the dojo. It'll seem weird to the other kids."

"That might be true," Ms. Platt admitted. "But also remember what I told you about the kiai: it's a spirit yell, so actually, it can be any word. Try 'hey.' And always kiai with your eyes. Like this."

She shouted, "Hey!" and gave us a laser stare so fierce we had to laugh.

"But I thought you said we should have a neutral expression," Samira said.

"Sometimes yes," Mrs. Platt agreed. "And sometimes no. Completely depends on the circumstance. If you want to defuse an emotional situation, use the neutral expression. If you're under attack, dominate with the eyes. All right, Mila, you're next. Ready?"

I nodded.

Her eyes met mine.

"What if some obnoxious kid makes a comment about how hot you look in yoga pants," Ms. Platt said.

"WHAT?" Jacob yelled.

"It's not Ms. Platt talking," another girl told him.

"Right, Gracie," Ms. Platt said calmly. "So, Mila? Is this obnoxious kid complimenting you? Verbally attacking? What do you think?"

"Verbally attacking?"

"Don't ask *me*. Trust your gut! Does Obnoxious Kid talking about your body that way *feel in your gut* like an attack?"

"Yeah, it does. Actually."

"So? Wanna respond, before he makes another obnoxious comment? Maybe something like, 'Hey, Mila, that Cookie Monster tee really fits your body.'"

Jacob fell over laughing. "Mila, you have a Cookie Monster tee?"

"No, I don't, and that's not the point, Jacob," I snapped.

"Well?" Ms. Platt said. She hadn't taken her eyes off my face. "What else ya got, Mila?"

"Um. I can walk away?"

"Is that a question? I said no questions."

"Sorry."

"And don't apologize!"

"Okay. So then I'm walking away." I took a step backward.

"Yeah, but don't," Ms. Platt said. "Better to take one step *toward* your verbal attacker. That tells him you're not going to cede turf. *Never cede turf.* And kiai with your eyes. Let's see it, Mila."

I took a step toward Ms. Platt, making angry eyes.

"Nice," said Ms. Platt. "And this time shout, 'Hey!' From way down deep in your stomach, not up high in your throat. No squeaking or squealing! I want to hear strong, authoritative voices, guys. And remember to spirit-yell with the eyes."

I took another step, shouting, "Hey!" and glaring as hard as I could.

"Awesome, Mila," Ms. Platt said. She gave me a high five. "Okay, guys, I want you all to practice this move ten times. Go."

We did. It felt good to be loud. Almost blue-sky good.

Ms. Platt beamed at us. "Truly excellent, guys! And you might want to practice this at home, too. I'd recommend in front of a mirror."

"Yeah, but these are all verbal attackers," Destiny protested. "What if the attack is physical?"

"Right." Ms. Platt took a breath. "Okay, so listen carefully. First thing I want to say about that is a line from *The Art of War* by Sun Tzu: 'The supreme art of war is to subdue the enemy without fighting.' Got that? *Without fighting.* Especially if there's a size or power difference with your attacker. So if you ever need to defend yourself physically, try to be like my cat Daisy."

"That's such a cute name," Gracie gushed. "Daisy."

"What *about* your cat, Ms. Platt?" Destiny asked impatiently.

"Okay. Whenever I need to take Daisy to the vet, she makes herself flat under my bed, like this." Ms. Platt dropped to the mat on her stomach, her arms and legs at crazy angles, as if she'd fallen from a stepladder. "I literally *cannot* get her to move. It drives me crazy, but it works. So if you're being physically attacked, try making yourself low to the ground. Flat and heavy."

"That's it?" Destiny looked doubtful.

"She also makes this horrible yowling sound. I'm sure you can hear her for miles around."

"Ms. Platt, you're saying we should *meow*? Instead of fighting back?"

"Isn't that why cats have claws? So they *can* fight back?" Samira argued.

"Yeah," Destiny said, nodding at Samira.

Ms. Platt stood again. "All right, listen, guys. Don't go home telling your parents I'm teaching you street fighting, or I'll get fired." She paused. "But in extreme cases, if you really, *really* have no choice, you can kick the attacker's shin with the side of your foot. It won't break any bones, or even hurt him much. But it *will* throw him off-balance. And the element of surprise can be extremely useful."

"Ooh, Ms. Platt, can we try that?" Jacob begged.

"If we do, it won't be a surprise," Samira told him.

"Even so, it's important to develop our muscle memory." Ms. Platt clapped her hands three times. "All right, guys, so line up and let's practice."

TRUMPET

At dinner, which we had at home that night, I couldn't stop talking about how great karate was, how cool Ms. Platt was, how she had a cat named Daisy who knew a special trick for avoiding the vet. How even though I knew we were only doing the class for the two-week introductory period, if there was any way we could sign up at E Motions for real, I would definitely want to take karate.

Mom was quiet as she ate her spaghetti. And suddenly I realized I'd gone too far.

"Although I know we can't afford it," I added. "I'm just saying *if*."

"Well, I'm just glad you found something you like, Mila," Mom said. She wiped her mouth with a napkin. "It's good to know things about yourself."

"Mommy, I really like dance about myself," Hadley announced.

"I know you do, baby." Mom's eyes looked tired.

Gah. Why did I say that about karate? Now she feels bad we can't pay for lessons.

"I'll clean the dishes," I said quickly.

"That's okay, sweetheart, I'll do it," Mom said. "You have homework and trumpet to practice."

"Oh right," I said. "Trumpet."

The thing about playing trumpet: it's really loud. So this means your mom can hear when you practice, and she can definitely hear when you don't. And unless you feel like explaining, *Yeah, there's no point practicing now that I'm in the back row of the trumpet section for a completely unfair reason that wasn't even my fault,* you need to open your music folder and work on "Pirate Medley."

Besides, not working on "Pirate Medley" would be— what had Ms. Platt called it? Ceding turf. Retreating. Admitting defeat. Telling Callum: *Okay, you win. I give up.*

And I wasn't ready to do that, wherever my chair was from now on.

So that evening I played the middle section until my lips were blubbery. I even got that blue-sky feeling by the end.

And afterward, in front of the mirror on my bedroom door, I did the self-defense moves Ms. Platt had taught us. A step toward the attacker, with laser eyes.

Hey.

Hey.

HEY!

LUNCHROOM

On Tuesday it rained—the kind of chilly, windy rain that made the trees sway, and meant we weren't allowed outdoors during lunch. So for the first twenty minutes of the period, my friends and I stayed in the lunchroom, breathing in fish tacos and pepperoni pizza, listening to Hunter Schultz and his friends at the next table yell at each other about some superhero game they were all playing on their phones.

Finally Zara stood. "I can't take this place one more second. I'm going to the chorus room. Who wants to come?"

"Not me," Max said, reading his phone.

"Me," Omi said. Immediately she looked at me. "Mila, you come too, okay?"

Obviously, she didn't want me to be alone, because she thought it wasn't safe. Also obviously, she hadn't mentioned the scorecard to Zara, or to anyone else, and I was grateful for that. Grateful that Omi was watching out for me.

But the idea of following Zara and Omi into the chorus room? Forget it. Because what was I supposed to do there, anyway? Sit there like a little kid being babysat while they sang scales? Better to stay in the lunchroom and breathe in fish tacos.

"You guys go ahead," I said. "Besides, I haven't even finished my yogurt."

I said this because I knew their chorus teacher, Ms. Goldenstein, went crazy if kids brought food into the chorus room.

"Come on, Omi," Zara said. "If I stay here, my head will explode."

"Mila, are you *sure*—" Omi began.

"Yep. See you later." I took a spoonful of yogurt to demonstrate that I was still eating.

She glanced over her shoulder at me as she and Zara left the table. I waved, to let her see I was fine.

And now it was just me and Max, who was typing something into his phone.

And laughing.

Typing something else.

Laughing again.

"Um," I said loudly.

He looked up. "Yeah?"

"Max, you're kind of ignoring me."

"Oh, sorry, Mila! I'm just talking to Jared."

"You mean you're texting each other? In here?"

Max nodded, blushing. "Yeah. He's eating over by the window, next to Liana."

"Well, that's ridiculous! You guys should have a conversation in person."

"I don't know."

"About what?"

Max blushed harder. "If he wants to. At his last school he was teased all the time."

"Max, just go over and sit with him! Don't be scared! Besides, aren't you two already friends?"

"Kind of. But in the lunchroom, in front of everyone . . ." He shrugged.

"You're not still afraid of Hunter, are you? Because he hasn't bothered you in forever. And Omi says he's changed, anyway."

"Maybe." Max chewed his lower lip thoughtfully. "Okay, Mila. Yeah, I think I will."

I watched Max get up from the table and walk across the lunchroom to sit next to Jared. Right away they were both talking and laughing.

I smiled, happy for my friend.

Although of course now I was all by myself.

SOLO

ut immediately I had this brilliant idea:

Since I'd spent so much time last night practicing "Pirate Medley," I'd go to the band room now, before class started. Maybe if I played that hard middle section, just me in the band room, playing a solo, Ms. Fender would hear it and reconsider sending me to the back row.

One more chance, Mila, she'd say. *Because you're a talented musician, and I can see you've been practicing. But if there any more conflicts—*

Oh, I promise there won't be, I'd tell her, putting on a musician face as serious as Callum's.

Except what happened was, when I got to the band room, she wasn't there.

All right, so just LEAVE, I told myself. But Ms. Platt's

voice was also in my head: *Take a step forward. Do not cede turf.*

How could I tell Max to be brave with Jared, and then run away like a coward?

And anyhow, Ms. Fender's fancy water bottle was on the desk, which meant she'd be back any minute.

I took my trumpet out of its case, wiped it, and began playing scales. Slowly, doing the longest notes I could.

B-flat, C, D, E-flat—

"Hey, Mila."

It shouldn't have jolted me, but it did. Callum's voice was in the room, coming from the doorway.

I kept playing, even though my hands started dripping and it was hard to breathe.

"Mila. *Mila.*"

He was coming toward me. I couldn't keep pretending not to hear.

"What?" I said over my shoulder.

Now he was standing in the row right in front of me. "You have to stop playing. I'm here to work with Ms. Fender on my solo."

"Well, she's not here right now, is she."

"Not yet. But she will be."

"Then I'll stop playing when she comes, all right?"

Don't ask questions! And don't cede turf!

I started playing again, super loud. B-flat, C, D, E-flat—

"MILA."

I could smell the pepperoni pizza he'd had for lunch as Callum took another step toward me, bumping the chair with his knee.

"You're not listening!" he said. "I need to warm up first, before she gets here. What about this don't you under-stand?"

I saw something in his eyes I'd never seen before. It looked almost like panic.

Then he grabbed my arm.

"HEY!" I shouted as I yanked my arm away.

And when I side-kicked him in the shin, Callum went sprawling, knocking over two chairs and three music stands on his way to the floor.

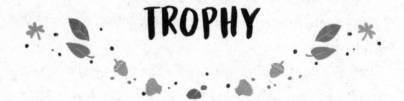

TROPHY

As he looked at us across his desk, Mr. McCabe's eyes were small and black. His pink cheeks sagged, like sofa pillows that had lost some stuffing. Up close like this, he seemed older than I'd realized, and tired.

"So can you explain to me what happened?" he asked. "Because I have to say I'm extremely surprised. At *both* of you."

Callum hunched his shoulders. "Nothing happened. Mila's so sensitive about everything these days, and she just went crazy for no reason!"

"That's a lie, and you know it," I snapped.

"All right," Mr. McCabe said. "Mila, can I hear from *you* why you kicked Callum?"

"Self-defense," I said.

"That's stupid," Callum muttered. "Because I didn't *do* anything."

"Yes you did! Of course you did! You grabbed my arm!"

"See? And you overreacted *again*."

Mr. McCabe steepled his thick pink hands. "Well, clearly there's some history here. What's been going on between the two of you?"

"Nothing," we both said at the same time.

Which would have been funny, if it were funny.

"Nothing?" Mr. McCabe repeated. Obviously he didn't believe us.

I pinched my wrist. Now was my chance to tell him the whole story. The hug and the bus and Tobias's hand on my butt and the sweater and the scorecard—

Except then my eyes focused on a small silver-colored trophy sitting on top of Mr. McCabe's bookshelf. JUNIOR BASKETBALL LEAGUE, SECOND PLACE.

This was Callum's team, and Leo's, and Dante's, and Tobias's. And of course Mr. McCabe was their coach.

I told myself that even if I said the truth, every single detail, he'd listen to the basketball boys over me. My friends had seen a few things, but not everything. I had no proof. I'd never even seen the stupid scorecard with my own eyes. And if people heard what I'd told Mr. McCabe (and of course they would, one way or the other), they'd never stop gossiping and teasing.

Plus, explaining Personal Body Stuff to the assistant principal . . .

No. It wasn't even possible to *imagine.*

"We just don't get along," I muttered.

"Not good enough," said Mr. McCabe, leaning back in his seat and crossing his arms on his chest. "And frankly, Mila, even if Callum did grab your arm, kicking his leg was simply wrong. Not how we resolve things around here."

"Overreaction," Callum repeated, avoiding my eyes.

SELF-CONTROL

After that, five things happened, and one didn't.

The things that happened:

I got a three-day after-school detention for kicking, which meant I couldn't go to karate starting Wednesday. And since our introductory offer to E Motions would expire next Thursday, that basically meant karate was over for me.

Callum got a one-day detention for grabbing my arm.

Neither of us was allowed on the blacktop the whole rest of the week.

Mr. McCabe made a rule for Callum and me: except when we were in class together, we couldn't be within twenty feet of each other. I guess he expected us to carry measuring tape in our pockets or something. But even if he did, I wasn't the one who needed it, because I wasn't the one who crowded, and bumped, and grabbed.

Also, he called Mom into school on Wednesday. This was the first time in my life she had ever been called in for my behavior, and my stomach hurt about it all day. Especially because I hadn't told Mom about the detention, and of course I knew Mr. McCabe would.

When she picked me up after detention, she pulled into the faculty parking lot and turned off the engine. "Mila, that boy had no business grabbing your arm, but you should have used words, you know? You just can't go around kicking kids in middle school! You could have seriously injured someone." She sighed. "Maybe missing karate is a good idea."

"No, no!" I cried. "It's not Ms. Platt's fault I kicked Callum! She told us *not* to fight! I just forgot, because I was so mad!"

"Well, but you *can't* forget, sweetheart. Self-control is so important, especially at school. And using words always works best anyway."

I don't know why this came out, but it did. "Is that how it went with Dad?"

"What?" She stared at me.

"I mean the other day, when you were on the phone with him. Did you win the argument with *words*?"

As soon as I said this, I knew I was wrong. Unfair to Mom, and fresh.

What was wrong with me? Maybe Zara was right—I was being too hard on everybody these days. Maybe I was turning into Dad, always saying the wrong things, hurting everyone's feelings. Especially Mom's.

"Sorry," I said immediately.

Mom's face pinched. "Mila, we're not discussing that," she said in a sharp, tight voice that didn't sound like her at all.

And she didn't say another word the whole ride home.

BACK

What didn't happen:

I didn't get kicked out of band, which I'd really thought might happen. Maybe Ms. Fender thought I'd been punished enough by having my seat changed and also getting detention. But what I really think was that she figured that if she made a big deal about me, she'd also have to punish Pet Number Three. And with the band concert coming up so soon, she needed to keep Callum focused.

Also, I was one of the only people who could play the middle section of "Pirate Medley" all the way through. So she needed me in the back row, and I think she knew it.

PROBLEM

The rest of that week at school, I kept looking over my shoulder, checking which boys were behind me. If they were walking too near me, or if their chairs were too close. If they were whispering or laughing at their phones. Or, even worse, taunting out loud.

A couple of times I heard "Ninja Warrior."

Once Dante called out, "Hey, Kickstarter!" And even though I didn't turn around, a bunch of boys started guffawing, anyway.

I also heard: "Footsie." "Steel Toe." "Legs." "Sidekick."

"Just ignore them," Samira told me in math class on Thursday, when the two of us were paired up to solve a geometry problem. "They don't even know what a real side kick *is*. And when are you coming back to karate?"

I shrugged. "I can't this week. Because of detention."

"Yeah, I heard. So what about next week?"

"I don't know."

"*Why* don't you know?" She'd answered her part of the math problem, and pushed the paper toward me.

I sighed. "It's complicated."

"Come on, Mila, it can't be *that* complicated."

The thing was, lately I'd been feeling exposed, like I was walking around school with the top layer of skin rubbed off. So even though this wasn't a subject I ever talked about, not even to my best friends, telling Samira the truth right then didn't feel like such a weird thing to do.

"We just have a week left for free classes," I said under my breath. "And my mom lost her job, so we can't afford it after that."

Samira nodded slowly. "Your mom should talk to Erica."

"What for? She's still going to make us pay for classes."

"Well, but Erica's really nice. I think if your mom goes to her and explains—"

"Samira, she *won't*. She's too embarrassed."

"Okay, so then maybe *you* should talk to Erica."

"Me?"

"Samira and Mila, have you solved the problem?" Ms. Fisher asked sharply as she walked around the classroom.

"*I* have but *she* hasn't," Samira replied, flashing me a look through her blue glasses.

SCORECARD

The only good part of that week was that Zara and Omi ate with me every day in the lunchroom. I knew they really wanted to go out to the blacktop, and I tried to tell them they didn't have to stay indoors just because I was being punished.

But Zara said, "Are you crazy, Mila? Why would we go outside and have fun, when we could be stuck in here with you, smelling fish sticks?"

"And Lysol," Omi added, laughing.

"Eww, and broccoli. Omigod, of all smells, that's the *worst*."

Max sat with Jared on Wednesday and Thursday, which made me feel a teeny bit bad. But on Friday they both joined our table. I'd never talked to Jared before;

he seemed nice, the way he laughed at everyone's jokes and told Omi he'd liked her story in ELA. He even said he played oboe, and was switching from orchestra to band. And for a few minutes I felt happy, because instead of our Circle of Friendship shrinking, the way I'd worried it might be, it actually seemed to be growing.

Until out of nowhere Jared said: "By the way, Mila, I'm really sorry about that scorecard thing."

Omi's eyes met mine.

I felt hot all over, then cold.

Crap.

"What scorecard thing, Jared?" Zara asked. "What are you talking about?"

Jared looked at Max, confused. "I thought you said everyone—"

"*No,*" Max told him, his blue eyes very wide and meaningful. "*Not* everyone."

"Oh. Oops."

"*What* scorecard thing?" Zara repeated. "Guys? Is there something I don't know about?"

I put down my Swiss cheese sandwich and leaned across the table so I could speak as quietly as possible. "Zara, it's just this stupid game the boys are playing. On their phones. About me."

She frowned. "What kind of game?"

"It's not an actual *game,*" Max said. "Not a *real* one."

"Well, if it's not a real game, what *is* it?" Zara's voice was rising.

"I haven't seen it; I've only heard about it," I said helplessly. "They get points for contact, apparently."

"What do you mean, 'contact'?"

"Come on, Zara, you know. Touching. Grabbing."

"Also for saying things," Max added. "About Mila's body. It's just gross."

Omi stared at her lap.

Of course Zara noticed. She eyed me, then Omi again. "So how come you guys never told me about it?"

I didn't answer.

"Mila just wanted to keep it private," Omi murmured.

"*Private?* How is it private if everyone knows except *me*?" Zara's voice wobbled.

"I think it's just the boys who know, probably," I said quickly. "Possibly one or two other people. And I didn't mean to hurt you, Zara. But it's really embarrassing. And sometimes the way you act—"

"*How?* How do I act?"

"Guys, *please* don't do this here," Omi begged. She jerked her thumb at the next table, where Ainsley, Liana, and a few other girls were sitting. And eavesdropping, most likely.

But I had to keep talking, or I'd explode. "You just make everything about *you*, Zara. Like you think you're a good friend, you really do, but the whole time it's just about *your* feelings, *your* opinions, no one else's. And to be honest, you're doing it right now!"

"It's true, Zara," Omi blurted. "You aren't actually thinking *about Mila.*"

Zara's eyes popped. Her mouth made a small O, like she was drinking from an invisible straw. "Yeah? Well, Mila, obviously you don't trust me with personal information. So too late about not hurting."

She got up and ran away from the table. Omi threw me a look as she ran after her.

So here we go again, I thought. *Circle of Friendship. Expand, contract, expand, contract.*

A temporary pebble O that just keeps on getting wrecked.

"You know, Mila, you really should tell Mr. McCabe," Max said.

I shrugged. I definitely didn't want to start *that* again. Not now. Even if it meant Max would just be mad at me too.

I saw Max catch Jared's eye.

"Mila, I'm really sorry—" Jared began.

"Not your fault," I told him, sighing.

ICE CREAM

Friday afternoon was my last detention. When Mom picked me up in the faculty parking lot, she leaned over and kissed my cheek.

"Tough week, sweetheart, but it's all over now," she said. "How about some ice cream in town?"

"That would be great, Mom! Thanks!" After that scene at lunch with Zara, I hadn't been able to finish my cheese sandwich, and now I was starving. "But only if you get some too."

"Okay, if you insist," Mom said, smiling. "Maybe some frozen yogurt."

She turned on the radio and drove us down Main Street.

And I guess all that detention this week had thrown

off my mental calendar, because I totally forgot that the Friday Thing would be happening in town.

So it hit me like a punch in the stomach to see Zara and Omi in front of Pie in the Sky Pizza. Talking and laughing with a bunch of kids—Ainsley, Daniel, Luis. A few others whose backs were to me as we drove by. But I was pretty sure I recognized two of them: Leo and Callum.

Best friends. Hanging out with worst enemies.

Even if they didn't plan it, how could Zara and Omi do this to me?

And of course this meant Zara had forgiven Omi for sticking up for me at lunch. Even though probably she was still mad at *me*.

And why was Omi here, acting like nothing had ever happened?

"Mom, let's just go home now," I begged. "Please."

"Seriously?" She turned to me. "No double-scoop cookie dough on a sugar cone? With sprinkles? What happened?"

"Nothing."

Mom turned off the radio. "Sweetheart, no one says yes to ice cream and a second later changes their mind for no reason. What's going on?"

"Mom, I'm just really tired and I want to go home. Please, can we just—"

"No, Mila, you need to tell me. Is everything okay with your friends?"

It was the question she was always asking, one way or the other, and I was always avoiding. But maybe it was time to answer.

"I don't know," I said. "It just feels like everything between us keeps getting messed up. And every time I think it's all fixed, it just gets messed up again."

I thought Mom might start asking a bunch of follow-up questions that I really didn't want to answer: *Is Zara being mean? Is Omi showing off?* But she surprised me.

"Sweetheart, have you talked to your friends?" she said quietly. "Do they understand how you feel?"

"I guess," I said. "I mean, I *tried*. . . ."

"People don't always hear the first time. Or they hear, but they don't actually *listen*. So it's up to you to tell them again."

"What if you keep saying the same things over and over, and they just *won't* listen?" I hadn't meant to turn the conversation to the basketball boys, but somehow here we were.

"Then you need to find a way to speak their language." Mom reached over and stroked my cheek. "Without kicking," she added.

WALK

It wasn't much of a Saturday. Mom spent the whole day on her computer, applying for jobs. And because it was raining, she let Hadley watch cartoons, so at least I could finish my homework and practice trumpet. By evening I'd just about mastered the last part of "Pirate Medley," and I was feeling pretty good about that. Even if nobody would hear me from the back row of the trumpet section.

I have to admit that once or twice that day, I almost texted Zara to apologize about what I'd said in the lunchroom. But before I could type words like *Sorry I didn't tell you about the scorecard thing*, or *Sorry I haven't shared Every Single Detail*, I stopped myself. Because I kept hearing Ms. Platt's voice: *Trust your gut.*

And if I'd asked my gut for advice on how to handle Zara, I knew my gut would answer: *Mila, are you crazy? Why are you even asking this question? You know you can't count on Zara.*

Besides, in the lunchroom, even Omi had accused Zara of not thinking about my feelings. Omi, who never took sides, never challenged Zara about anything.

Well, except for that time outside CVS, when Zara had insisted on yelling at the boys. Omi *had* taken my side then, begging Zara to listen to me.

Also, after that time by the lockers when Tobias grabbed my butt. Zara said I didn't understand about flirting, and Omi *did* tell Zara she wasn't being fair. She'd said it in her quiet little voice, but she'd said it.

And really, about the scorecard: Omi *could* have kept it to herself. She didn't *have* to tell me about it, if she didn't want to start a big fuss—and of course she *could* have blabbed to Zara behind my back. I mean, if all she'd cared about was avoiding fights, and keeping Zara happy.

I'd never thought about it this way before, but Omi was brave. It wasn't fair of me to feel weird that she'd gone into town with Zara yesterday. And standing in front of the pizza place with Leo and Callum—it didn't mean anything. She could stand anywhere, with anyone she wanted. She was a true friend, really.

As for Max—well, I wasn't mad at him, and I was glad he'd found Jared. But it kind of seemed like I'd gone blurry on him lately. Like maybe he'd forgotten we were supposed to be friends.

Or he'd decided the weirdness was too much, and he didn't want to deal with it anymore.

On Sunday morning, Mom was back on her computer at the dinette table, and Hadley needed attention, so that meant me. This was incredibly annoying, because I was trying to read in the living room, and she was in one of her moods where she just kept asking *Whyyyyyy*. Like:

Hadley: Mila, *whyyyy* can't we go to the dog park?

Me: Because it's raining.

Hadley: We can take umbrellas! And I can wear my new pink rain boots!

Me: Yes, but Delilah hates the rain.

Hadley: *Whyyyy?*

Me: I don't know, Hadley. Ask Delilah.

Hadley: Mila, don't you understand? How many times do I have to explain this? Delilah can't answer because she CAN'T TALK!

Me: . . .

Seven minutes later:

Hadley: Mila, can we go to the park *now*?

Finally, around two o'clock, I told Mom I couldn't deal with Hadley anymore, so she called Mrs. Ames and Cherish to come over. At first I wasn't sure what the point of this was, because Cherish didn't seem like much of a playmate. But then I could hear Mom in the kitchen, speaking to Mrs. Ames in that half-whisper, half-murmur voice moms use when they don't want kids to eavesdrop:

Mom: I'm starting to get really worried, Everyone who responds says they want a reference from my old boss, but I'm afraid to give it!

Mrs. Ames: Why, Amy? Do you really think he'd say bad things about you?

Mom: I honestly don't know what he'd say. But yeah, the way he reacted when I said I was quitting, I wouldn't put it past him.

Hearing this made my insides freeze. It was bad enough not being able to afford E Motions, and barely any new clothes, and having to watch every penny we spent at the supermarket. But if Mom couldn't get a new job, we could lose our little house. And possibly even starve.

Well, I wasn't going to sit here and let that happen.

"Mom, I'm taking Delilah out for a walk," I called out from the hallway.

"But it's raining out," she called back.

"It's okay—I'll take an umbrella. We can't be stuck indoors all weekend!"

"I wanna come too," Hadley yelled from the living room. "With my pink rain boots!"

And because by then my heart was banging and my head was buzzing, I agreed.

ERICA

ren't we going to the dog park?" Hadley asked as we stopped in front of E Motions.

We both huddled under my umbrella. "Maybe afterward. I think Delilah wants to get out of the rain for a little. So let's go inside, and I'll go talk to Erica."

"The lady with the arms? What about?"

"You'll see."

Hadley liked riddles and puzzles, so this answer actually worked for her. "But what about Delilah? I think probally they don't let wet dogs inside."

I hadn't thought this through until right now. "Well, Hadley, that's why you're extremely important. You'll stay here with Delilah in the lobby. And you're in charge of her behavior, so don't let her sit on anything, or pee, okay? I'll go look for Erica and be back in a minute."

I pushed open the front door before Hadley could protest, and Delilah zoomed inside, happy to escape the rain. Right away she shook herself off, spattering raindrops and dog fur.

"*Bleh!*" Hadley yelled.

"Stay," I commanded. "Both of you!"

E Motions had the whole second floor, so I ran upstairs. Because it was Sunday afternoon, and rainy, the reception area was packed with kids and grown-ups desperate for something to do, I guessed.

A sweaty-foot smell attacked my nose.

I grabbed a *Yourself* magazine and sat on the floor.

After about two minutes, Erica raced by. Her blond hair was slipping out of her ponytail, and she seemed even more frazzled than usual.

"Three o'clock sessions are about to begin!" she called out. "If anyone still needs to see me about signing up—"

Three women, one holding a screaming baby, surrounded Erica as she typed things into her phone. When they finally finished, and everyone had left the reception area for their classes, Erica waved at me. So I stood.

"Hey there, Mila," she said. "You guys disappeared on us. Is your mom okay? I wasn't sure if there was a problem . . . ?"

"No. No problem," I lied. "I know Mom's been trying

to talk to you about signing up and everything. But you're always so busy, and she can never find you here."

"Oh, really? Sorry about that! You know, I used to have an office manager—"

"Yeah, you told us. I bet that made everything so much easier."

Erica laughed. I think she was surprised at me for saying this. "Oh, it certainly did. Yes, absolutely!"

"You probably wish you had another—"

Hadley picked that exact moment, just as I was getting started, to burst into the reception area with Delilah tugging on the leash, excited by all the sweaty-foot smells.

"Sorry, Hadley honey, no dogs allowed up here," Erica called out.

Hadley's face crumpled. "But I was downstairs all by myself for *hours*! Mila, you said you'd be back in *a minute*. 'A' means 'one.'"

"Yes, but I told you I needed to find Erica," I said. "Sorry it took so long, but Erica was *super busy*. And there wasn't anyone else here to ask for help." I turned to Erica. "Too bad you have to do everything yourself."

Erica did a weak smile. "Anyhow, please tell your mom to stop by again; I'm always here, someplace or other. And now, girls, if you'll please take the dog back outside—"

"Hey, I just thought of something!" I told Erica. "Would you *want* someone to help you? If the person was nice, and smart, and super experienced in . . . office stuff, and really loved coming here all the time?"

"Help? You mean as a job?"

I nodded, holding my breath.

"Wait!" Hadley shouted. "I know who she could hire! MOM."

Erica blinked a few times. "Girls, is your mom looking for work? Because seriously, if she is, I'd love to chat with her."

I shot my little sister a spirit yell from the eyes. This one meant DO NOT SPEAK ON PENALTY OF DEATH.

"Well, I'm not exactly sure, but I can ask," I said casually.

Then I yanked Delilah's leash and grabbed Hadley's hand, and the three of us zoomed out of the building.

Of course, the second we got back home, Hadley blurted out what Erica had said. I was afraid Mom would be mad at me, considering that she never talked about how her job search was going, and had only told Mrs. Ames about her boss when she thought I wasn't listening.

But Mom actually seemed excited. "Did Erica say she'd call me? Or did she want me to call her?"

"She just said she'd like to talk to you," I said. "I really don't know anything else."

"Okay. Wow." Mom couldn't stop smiling as she shook

her head. "This is *not* what I was expecting *at all*. I thought you said you were just going to the dog park."

"Well, it was raining, so we stopped into E Motions. And Erica was there." I was careful not to lie, because I knew Mom was watching my face closely.

"Okay, but how did it even come up? I mean, what did you say to her?"

I gave Mom a hug. "I just think maybe I spoke her language," I said.

MAX

By Monday morning the sun finally came out, and everyone was cheery and chatty at breakfast, even me. Mom wasn't talking about it, but I knew she'd be seeing Erica at noon. The biggest, most important thing would be her getting a job . . . but I couldn't help thinking that if she *did*, I'd get to go back to karate.

If, if, if.

My stomach was fluttery, but in a good way.

Butterflies, not moths.

And I refused to be upset when Zara wasn't waiting for me before homeroom. Instead I walked down the hall to hang out with Max before the bell rang, listening to him go on and on about that phone game he was playing with Jared.

Until I couldn't stand hearing about it anymore. "Max, I'm really happy for you," I interrupted.

His blue eyes widened. "About what?"

"That you're such good friends with Jared now."

He took a second. "Well, Mila, you know it's all because of you."

"Me?"

"Yeah, you were the one who made me go sit with him in the lunchroom. If you hadn't—"

He cut himself off. I guessed it was because right then, Liana and Ainsley were walking by, giving us a drowsy Monday sort of wave as they entered homeroom.

We waved back.

"If I hadn't, what?" I asked as soon as they were inside.

"Never mind," Max said. He blew out some air.

I decided to keep going.

"Max, are you mad at me?" I blurted. "Because it seems like you're sort of avoiding me. And when we do hang out, you're barely talking."

Max shifted his backpack. I could tell he was planning his answer.

"All right, Mila, you really want to hear?" he said after a few seconds. "You're always giving me advice. Like: Go sit with Jared. Go tell Mr. McCabe about Hunter. And I listen to you because you're my friend, and you're right about things, usually. But when I tell you to do something, you don't."

I stared at him. "Is this about the scorecard? Because you told me to tell Mr. McCabe?"

"Well, yeah. But also about all that *other* stuff with those boys. I told you it was bullying, and you just ignored me. And now it's gotten worse, and I don't know what you want me to do about it!"

I looked past Max's shoulder, down the hall. Ms. Wardak was scolding some kid, a sixth grader.

"I don't want you to do anything, Max," I said softly. "It's my problem anyway."

His eyebrows rose. "Would it help if I came with you to Mr. McCabe? Because I will."

I shook my head.

Max hadn't taken his eyes off my face. "Why not? Are you scared?"

Was I? "Scared" was such a strong word. And so negative.

Max tilted his head toward me. His voice was quiet, almost a whisper. "You know, Mila, when Hunter was bothering me last year, you *made* me tell Mr. McCabe. I didn't want to, but you wouldn't leave me alone about it! And afterward I was glad I did, because Hunter totally ignores me now."

"Max, that was different!"

"How? How was it different?"

"A lot of ways! Because it was one kid who was just

saying things. And Mr. McCabe wasn't his basketball coach." I took a sharp breath. "Also."

"Also what?"

"Because this stuff—what's been happening to *me*—is just extremely hard to talk about," I said. "*Especially* to Mr. McCabe. I mean, thanks for offering, Max, I really appreciate it. But I know you think it's just bullying, and it's *not*."

Max's face tightened. "What happened to me wasn't 'just bullying' either. And you think it was *easy* telling Mr. McCabe I was being called gay? Like it was an *insult*?"

"Sorry," I said immediately. My face was hot; I could tell this was coming out all wrong. Why was everything I said such a disaster? "I *know* it wasn't easy for you, Max," I added, my voice croaking now. "Please believe me, okay? And it's not what I meant, anyway! I just meant this stuff with me is *different*. And I definitely wouldn't call it regular bullying."

"So what *would* you call it, then?"

I opened my mouth to answer.

But I didn't have any words.

Because all the words I could think of—*bullying, teasing, flirting*—seemed too simple, too small, to hold all the hurt I was feeling.

UNTAG

When lunchtime came, I got a hummus-on-pita and a chocolate chip cookie, went out to the blacktop, and looked around. No surprise that none of my friends were waiting over by the pebbles. Zara was under the basketball hoop passing a ball to Liana and Ainsley, while Omi chatted nearby with Daniel Chun. No sign of Max and Jared. No sign of the basketball boys, which was a little weird.

Okay—and what am I supposed to do now?

I walked once around the perimeter of the blacktop, nibbling the chips off the cookie, counting the length and width by the number of times my sneakers touched the asphalt.

Maybe if Mom gets the job, I can finally get new sneakers. . . .

When I'd made it to the pebbles, Samira jumped out at me. "MILA," she shouted. "YOU ARE HEREBY SUMMONED."

I was so startled I laughed. "To what?"

"THE GAME OF UNTAG, YOU FOOL." She grinned. "You know how to play?"

"Not really."

"Well, haha, neither do I!"

She started to explain some stuff, though—how Lily Sherman was Grand Master, which meant she had a power called "morph." If you were "cornered" by three "squires," you were "neutralized," which meant you were "dormant" for the rest of the lunch period. Unless you were "zapped" by one of two "red dragons"—

"Hold on," I said. "What exactly does 'cornered' mean?"

"You're surrounded on three sides at a distance of three arms' lengths. There's no touching; that's why it's untag. Although if a troll summons you from behind . . ."

"Oh," I said. "Uh-huh."

She kept explaining, but I'd stopped following. All I was thinking was: *Samira is nice. I don't care how to play this crazy game. Great that there's no touching. And woohoo, I'm not by myself!*

"Okay, got all that?" she finally asked.

"No," I admitted.

"Well, just fake it. That's what I do. AND NOW MAKE

HASTE, GREEN RAPTOR!" she shouted. "THESE PARTS ARE DARK AND FILLED WITH DANGER."

"Wait, what?" I shouted back.

But she ran away.

I was a green raptor? Why green? Did I have any powers? She hadn't mentioned any, so maybe not.

But whatever. At least now I had something to do.

So I started running.

DEAL

Running felt good, because it meant not thinking.

I mean, I had no idea *where* I was running, or *why*, or even who the other players were. Samira had disappeared on me. But Max and Jared both seemed to be playing—at least, when I waved at them across the blacktop, they both made excited arm motions that looked like *KEEP MOVING! DON'T STOP!*

So okay, I just kept going.

But after a few minutes of nonstop running across the blacktop in a sort of figure eight, my lungs were burning and I had a sharp cramp in my side.

A quick time-out won't matter, I told myself. *And who cares if it does.*

I slipped behind a tree, just over the edge of Not-School.

Almost immediately, I was surrounded on three sides—
by Hunter, Luis, and Callum.

Wait. *Callum?* Why was he playing untag, anyway?

And what were the rules again if you were surrounded?
My brain was blank.

"HEY," I said. It came from my throat, so I did it again,
this time from my stomach. "HEY."

"Hey *what*?" Hunter smiled, but it wasn't friendly. "You
can't speak, Mila. You're being neutralized."

"How come? You guys are . . . squires?"

"We're flamethrowers," Luis said. "And we're officially
taking you prisoner. You have to come with us." He clamped
his hand on my shoulder.

My heart banged.

I'm their prisoner?

But no. I can't be.

I shoved his hand away. Too hard, but I didn't care.
"Don't you touch me, Luis! I'm not going!"

He seemed surprised. "This is not a choice."

"And don't talk to me like that!"

"Silence. You do not get to dictate the terms of capture—"

"No, wait," Callum said in his normal voice, not in
the booming untag sort of voice the other boys were
using.

"Wait for *what*?" Luis demanded. He seemed annoyed.

"Mila and I made a deal with Mr. McCabe. She has to

keep twenty feet away from me all the time, except in class. So actually, she shouldn't even *be* here."

My face burned. I felt raw, exposed. "Callum, it's supposed to work *both* ways. So also *you* have to keep twenty feet from *me*."

"No, Mila, we made the agreement because of how *you* attacked *my leg*. In case you forgot."

"Oh, I remember perfectly!"

"Aww, never mind, Callum," Hunter said impatiently. "Let's just go—"

But Callum wouldn't stop. "Yeah, Mila, technically you shouldn't even be playing. Because there's no way we can enforce the twenty-foot rule in a game like this, where everyone is always moving around, right? So unless you want Ms. Wardak to report you to Mr. McCabe—"

"Oh, fine!" I exploded. "Who cares about this stupid game anyway!"

"I think you do," Callum said, looking me right in the eye.

RETREAT

I can't even describe how mad I felt, leaving the blacktop. Walking away from a game I didn't understand, and hadn't even wanted to play. Being humiliated by Callum in front of people who weren't my friends. Ceding turf.

But I knew I had no choice. Callum was right—we weren't supposed to be near each other outside class. Within twenty feet, according to McCabe. And if Callum was going to play that stupid untag game, there was no way to avoid him every minute, unless I spent the entire lunch period running away from him, and how much fun would that be?

And why was this even happening? Because I wouldn't let Callum crowd my chair? Because I called him out for making comments about my sweater, and my butt? Kicked his shin? Embarrassed him in front of Mr. McCabe?

All he'd gotten was a one-day detention, anyway; Mr. McCabe had basically ignored Callum's *action*, and only focused on my *reaction*. Just like Ms. Fender had banished me to the back of the trumpet section and let Callum still have his solo.

It was all so incredibly *wrong and unfair*.

But the last thing I wanted was another meeting with Mr. McCabe, followed by more detention, or something even worse.

So I needed to get off the blacktop now. Keep moving.

And go where?

I'd just stepped inside the building when Samira grabbed my elbow.

"Hey—what happened?" she asked breathlessly. "I thought you were playing."

"I can't," I said.

"Why not?"

I told her about Callum—the twenty-foot rule. How he'd never let me forget it, which meant I couldn't do the game. Or anything else on the blacktop, really.

"So you're just going to let him push you around like that?" Her eyes flashed behind her glasses.

"Mr. McCabe said if we break the twenty-foot rule, there'll be another consequence. A bigger one."

"Oh, Mila." She shook her head. "This is really bad. If it were *me*—"

"But it isn't." I could hear that it came out sharper than I meant it. "Sorry."

"Don't apologize; you're right, I shouldn't have said that. It's just so . . . frustrating! Where are all your friends? Zara, Omi, Max . . ."

I shrugged. "The whole thing is out of control."

"Yeah. Well, it needs to stop."

"How?"

"I don't know. But you can't do it alone. Where are you going now?"

I shrugged again.

"Fine, then let's go to the band room together. Band starts in thirteen minutes; we can practice for the concert."

Now I groaned. "Samira, I've already practiced like crazy. No one will hear me from the back row anyway."

"Sure they will, Mila. You're louder than you think you are." She poked her finger into my elbow and grinned. "And if the band room is empty, we'll practice our kicks."

JOB

Hanging out with Samira in the band room made me feel a whole lot better. Not only did we play our parts in "Pirate Medley," but we also practiced overhead blocks, forward punches, and side kicks. And Samira saved me a seat on the bus going home, so even though it was Monday, and the basketball boys weren't even there, I wasn't sitting alone. She did ask if I was going to karate again; I didn't want to jinx anything, so I didn't tell her about Mom's meeting with Erica.

A few minutes after I got home, Mom and Hadley walked in the door with Mrs. Ames and Cherish. As soon as Mom saw me, she shouted: "GUESS WHAT, MILA."

"You got the job?"

"I GOT THE JOB."

She'd be Erica's office manager, she said, taking care of all the paperwork, answering phones, basically running the place so Erica could teach fitness classes.

"The pay isn't great," Mom admitted. She was beaming, happier than I'd seen her in weeks. Maybe months. "But it's a place I absolutely love. And of course now we can take unlimited classes—"

Hadley screamed and clapped and jumped.

"And I owe it all to my girls," Mom continued, gathering Hadley and me in a hug. "This is *our* job. The three of us did it together."

"Aww," Ms. Ames said. "Hold that pose!" She snapped a photo of us with her phone.

"Don't forget Delilah," Hadley said. "She helped too. If she didn't hate the rain so much, probally we wouldn't have gone into E Motions."

"Yeah," I lied. "It was really a team effort." I snuggled inside Mom's arms, needing that hug more than I wanted to say, especially in front of Mrs. Ames.

Right then Hadley jumped up and hit me in the chin. "Mommy, *now* can I get a hamster named Budget?"

Mom laughed. "I'll need to think about that, baby."

"'Think about' means okay!"

"It does not," I said. "It means—"

"Mila, I heard! You don't have to *tell* me! But also can we *please* go to Junior Jay's?" Hadley was still jumping.

"Okay with you, sweetheart?" Mom asked me. "We could even go to E Motions first, and afterward, maybe Molly and Cherish could join us for supper? My treat," she added.

"Oh, Amy, you don't have to," Mrs. Ames protested.

"Well, but I insist. You've been such a help."

Suddenly Mom looked at me with eyes that were asking something, but I couldn't tell what. Maybe the question was: *Are you okay with this, Mila? Because I know how you feel about Molly—*

I just smiled at her.

"Sure," I said. "Let's celebrate."

PROGRESS

I got through the rest of that week by practicing karate, thinking about karate, going to karate after school every day. Ms. Platt seemed really happy I was back in class, complimenting me on doing stronger kicks and punches, quicker blocks.

Soon Ms. Platt paired me up with Destiny, the most advanced student in the class. And every time Ms. Platt passed us, she'd correct an elbow or a knee and then comment, "Progress, Ms. Brennan."

Hearing that word—"progress"—made me crazy happy.

Even I could see progress when I watched myself practice in the mirror. Now I was doing the moves smoothly, one after the other, without hesitating or needing to catch my breath.

But was my body any different? Probably not, after just a few lessons. But somehow, in some way I couldn't describe, it *felt* different. More solid. Sharper and just more . . . *there*.

Could other people tell?

On Friday I got an answer. At dismissal, Samira asked me to get a slice of pizza with her in town. My first thought was: *Oh no. Because what if the basketball boys are there?*

My second thought: *Okay, so what if they are?* They hadn't been bothering me lately: not like they'd forgotten about me—every once in a while, I caught Callum peeking at me in band—but more like they were taking a time-out.

But still, at least for now, they'd backed off. And anyhow, I'd be with Samira, who I knew scared them whenever she glared through her blue glasses and flipped her long braids like a whip.

"Sure," I told her.

It surprised me how happy she looked.

We walked into town together. She told me about her bratty little brother; I told her about my bratty little sister. We both complained about how much our moms expected us to do around the house. She told me about her lazy old cat; I told her about our lazy old dog.

When we got to Pie in the Sky Pizza (*no boys, woohoo!*),

we each got a slice and a can of Sprite. And then Samira said how unfair she thought Ms. Fender was being about my chair in band.

"You should speak up about it," she said.

"Nah, Ms. Fender won't listen," I replied. "She's made up her mind about me."

"People change," Samira insisted. "Look how much *you* have."

"Me?"

"Yeah, Mila, you." She took a sip out of her can. "You're so much stronger now. Your moves are amazing, really. And you even *look* bigger too."

I grinned so hard at that, some Sprite leaked out of my mouth.

And suddenly it felt like everything was changing.

Mom's job meant she was happy, and didn't even bother fighting with Dad about money. Hadley was happy too, busy with dance and gymnastics. So overall, things at home were calmer.

The friend situation was more complicated.

Zara met me outside homeroom every morning, and we chatted pretty much the way we used to, but never about anything important, and not for very long. And she was playing basketball almost every lunch now, mostly with Liana and Ainsley, sometimes even with the boys. This was fine with me, actually: I didn't want us to *not* be friends anymore. But after everything that had happened between us, I was feeling shaky about her, to be honest.

Once, when the two of us were the first out on the blacktop, I even tried apologizing for not telling her about the scorecard.

"Eh, already forgot that whole thing," she said, flicking her hand at me. A second later she grabbed a basketball and started dribbling.

I tried to think if this was good or bad:

She forgot because she's forgiven me.

She forgot because it was never that important to her.

I mean, Zara was Zara. She'd always *be* Zara, keeping me off-balance, unsure. And now I knew not to expect any different.

I was afraid things would stay shaky with Max, too—but somehow they didn't. He never mentioned Mr. McCabe to me again. Or the word "bullying." It was like we'd agreed to be friends *despite* those topics. Which was tricky to do, but we were both trying.

Sometimes during lunch Omi watched Zara play basketball, and sometimes she hung out with Max, Jared, and me (that is, when Max and Jared weren't playing untag, or I wasn't chatting with Samira). But even when we weren't together on the blacktop, or inside the building,

I always knew Omi had an eye out for me—paying attention in her own quiet way.

One lunch period she gave me a flat, brown-speckled shell from her collection.

"It's a limpet shell," Omi explained. "Scientists think it's the strongest biological material in the world. Stronger than a spider's web."

"What's a limpet?" I asked her.

She smiled. "A tiny mollusk, like a snail. They're very common; you see them all over ocean rocks. Tía Rosario brought this one back for me from Puerto Rico. But I was thinking it should be yours, Mila. Because it's so tough."

I threw my arms around Omi and hugged her tight.

The Circle of Friendship wasn't wrecked forever, I told myself. But maybe it was sort of a squishy egg shape now. And maybe something else was taking its place.

SHIRT

Two weeks later was the fall concert.

It was weird how nervous I felt, considering I didn't have a solo. But I guess all the weeks of practicing, plus the sight of parents filling the auditorium, plus wearing the concert outfit (white shirt, black skirt or pants, black shoes that weren't sneakers) added up to a fluttery stomach. Would I be able to do my best onstage—ignore all the buzzing in my head, all the noisy distractions, and just hear the beautiful blue sky of my trumpet?

I wanted to believe I could, but as I walked into the band room, I wondered.

"Omigod, did you see all the people out there?" Annabel said, practically attacking me at the door. Her eyes were huge.

We were supposed to wait there until it was our turn to go on. First the orchestra performed, then the chorus, then us. More time for us to develop stage fright.

"What if some people leave before we go on?" Jared asked.

"Their loss," Samira said, flicking her hand. "I'd rather play for a small audience that actually *listens*."

Samira sounded confident, the way she always did, but I spotted tiny beads of sweat on her upper lip. If *she* was nervous, how was everyone else supposed to feel?

"Hey, Callum!" Leo shouted. "You forgot something!"

"What?" Callum asked. His face went pale.

"To wear pants! But your legs look so pretty in that skirt!"

"Ha, funny, Leo," Callum said.

Dante let out a whoop. "Yeah, man, you should wear skirts more often."

"Or a dress," Tobias said. "With a bra."

Samira flashed me a look. *Ignore them*, she mouthed.

I know, I mouthed back.

Just then Ms. Fender poked her head into the band room. She was wearing a fancy black silk dress with a deep V-neck. Not the sort of dress they sold at Old Navy.

"Five minutes, guys," she said. "Remember to walk out single file, and take your chairs without any talking. Also remember band posture: straight backs, open chests, feet on the floor. Soloists, you're all ready, so knock it out of the park. Don't hold back; this is your chance to let it all out."

She turned to leave.

"Ms. Fender, how will we know when it's time?" Annabel squealed.

"Try to stay calm, Annabel. I'll be back in two minutes to lead you out there. I just want to check that my music is ready onstage. Now please line up by section, okay?"

She walked off.

Samira nodded at me.

"You'll do great," I said.

"So will you. Really." She smiled. Then she wiped her upper lip with her pointer finger.

I watched her walk off to join the other clarinet players. Lily Sherman patted her on the back.

My heart was banging as I walked over to the trumpet kids.

"Dude, seriously, you're gonna blow the roof off," Dante was telling Callum.

"Yeah," Luis said. "You totally got this, bruh."

"Thanks," Callum said.

I chewed the inside of my cheek. That kind of cheering made this sound like a basketball game. And was I supposed to pep-talk Callum too? Well, forget it.

"All right, band, we're on!" Ms. Fender was back now. "Line up, and follow me! Good luck, everybody! Here we go!"

"Hey, Mila, time to line up," Tobias told me.

"Yeah, I heard," I said. "You don't need to tell me."

I walked to the back of the line.

Right away Callum was behind me. He was wearing a spicy deodorant, or something, and standing too close, the toes of his shoes hitting my heels.

Just ignore him.

Think about the big wide open blue sky.

Think about the big wide Not-School camera shot.

In a minute you'll be onstage—

"Hey, Mila," Callum murmured.

Look straight ahead. Band posture.

"Mila."

Kiai with the eyes—

"Hey, Mila, listen. *Mila.* You know what? I can see right through your shirt."

And after that all I heard was laughing.

PERFORMANCE

I think it was the timing.

Because I mean, there wasn't even any contact. It was only a bunch of stupid words.

But speaking *those* exact words just as we were going onstage? That was like saying: *You're about to embarrass yourself, Mila. Because if I can see through your shirt, so can the ENTIRE AUDIENCE.*

Or worse: *It doesn't matter how well you play, or how much you've practiced. All anyone will notice is what's under your shirt.*

So I guess the humiliation of being stuck in the back row mixed with everything else that had happened these past few weeks—it was too much. I couldn't get past Callum's stupid comment, plus all the laughing.

Especially the laughing.

Right then I knew that no way, however I played, however hard I focused on the music, would I get the beautiful open big blue-sky feeling.

Hey, Mila, I can see right through your shirt.

As if I were invisible.

But I wasn't. I was *there.*

And I could hear Samira's voice in my head: *You're louder than you think you are.*

As we took our seats onstage, the almost-full audience clapped and cheered. Mom and Hadley waved at me from the third row, but I didn't wave back.

Ms. Fender bowed—a music bow, not a karate bow—and beamed at the audience. "Good evening, friends and families," she said into her mic. "We're so happy to share with you all of our hard work so far this fall. I'm extremely proud of our seventh graders; I think we've really been coming together as a band these past few weeks, and I'm looking forward to a great year ahead! Our first piece this evening is called 'Pirate Medley,' and it features two of our most accomplished players, Samira Spurlock on clarinet and Callum Burley on trumpet."

Ms. Fender turned to us, smiled, and winked. She tapped her stand three times with her baton. "Ready, guys? A one and a two and a three—"

Samira's solo went great, as usual.

And when Callum stood for his, I played a B-flat. Really loud.

It was strange—like I was onstage and not-onstage, both at the same time. Floating above the stage, looking down. Or no—onstage but also in the audience, watching and listening. Wondering what would happen next.

"Mila, shut up," Dante hissed.

Callum turned his head to me. He looked shocked.

A few people in the audience nervous-giggled. They probably thought I wasn't paying attention, that I came in too soon.

Callum took a breath and started playing again. C, D, D, F-sharp—

I honked a C-sharp.

More people were laughing.

Ms. Fender leaned toward me frantically, trying to kiai me with her eyes. I refused to look.

Callum, blushing, started over. As if that was even allowed. And of course everyone knew it wasn't.

C, D, D, F-sharp—

I blasted an A-flat.

Now the laughing stopped. Instead there were murmurs. Onstage and in the auditorium.

"Go, Mila!" Zara shouted from the back. Someone else shouted, "Woohoo!" A couple of people started clapping.

Callum stood there, red-faced. I could see that his

brain had logged off, and he had no idea if he should start over a third time, or maybe just forget the whole thing and sit back down.

And then, with Callum still standing there frozen, someone squawked a long, loud note on the clarinet: Samira.

Followed by a screech on the saxophone: Annabel.

"All right, guys," Ms. Fender whispered fiercely. "That's enough—"

I blared an A.

Jared played a bunch of random oboe notes.

Hunter made a farting-dog sound on his trombone.

I did the trumpet version of a yowling cat.

Ms. Fender banged her baton. "THAT'S IT. EVERY-BODY, STOP. NOW."

She spun around to face the audience. "Ladies and gentlemen, this is obviously a prank, but please accept my apologies. I know many of you had to leave work early to be here, and . . . well, I just don't know what to say except I'm sorry for wasting your time. And now, please excuse us. *Seventh grade band, off this stage!*"

JOKE

Once when Hadley was about four years old, she flushed four cans of Play-Doh down the toilet, just to see what would happen. Mom's face when that happened was the angriest one I'd ever seen.

Until now.

Ms. Fender was so mad she was shaking. Her voice was shaking too. "Can someone please explain to me what happened onstage? The rudeness to a fellow band member? Sacrificing all of our hard work, in front of all the parents and the entire grade?"

"Yeah, Mila," Ainsley said. "My grandma drove for two hours to hear me play. So I'm really, really mad you did that!"

"Mila wasn't the only one," Annabel protested as she caught my eye.

"No, but she started it."

"Yeah, she definitely did," Daniel grumbled.

My stomach squeezed. My head felt like a balloon about to float away.

"I'm waiting for an answer to my question," Ms. Fender warned.

"It was just Mila being psycho," Dante said. "Overreacting the way she always does."

"To what?"

Silence.

"To *what*?" Ms. Fender repeated, her voice as sharp as broken glass.

"Callum said something to me," I said. My throat was so dry I could hear my voice croaking. "Right before we went onstage. It's been happening a lot lately, not just with him, and I didn't know what to do. But I guess I just . . . figured out how to speak his language."

Everyone was staring at me.

"So you needed to trash the performance," Dante said. "Not just for Callum. For the whole band."

"Anyhow, it was just a joke," Callum muttered.

"A *joke*?" Ms. Fender said. She looked at Callum, then at Dante, then at me. "What kind of joke?"

Nobody answered.

"*What kind of joke?*" she demanded.

"Mila just takes everything too seriously," Leo said. "She's way too sensitive."

"That's not true," I snapped. "You *know* it isn't, Leo."

"All right," Ms. Fender said. She suddenly seemed exhausted. "Can someone *please* help me out a little? I'm having a hard time understanding."

"Do you really want to hear, Ms. Fender?" Samira asked. "Because there's been stuff going on for a while. Everyone here knows about it. And if they say they don't, they're lying."

Liana did her blank face.

Samira shot a look at Hunter, who stared at the floor.

Then she raised her eyebrows at me. *Well?* Samira's eyes were saying.

I knew what Samira was urging me to do, but I couldn't. Not here, in front of everyone. That would just be more punishment. Humiliation.

I shook my head.

But now Ms. Fender wouldn't look away from me. "All right," she said. "Everyone, out of the band room. Mila, may I please speak to you in private?"

TEACHER

I told Ms. Fender the whole story, from the beginning. About the fuzzy green sweater, the hugging and the grabbing. What had happened at the lockers, on the bus, on the blacktop. When I told her all the stuff that had gone on in the band room, Ms. Fender's hand flew to her mouth.

"*Oh,*" she said. "Mila, I'm so sorry! I had no idea—"

"I know," I said.

Then I just kept going. I even told her about the score-card. At least, as much as I knew about it.

Which was pretty weird, because I'd always been a bit afraid of Ms. Fender, really. But I think maybe it had to do with being a musician: Ms. Fender turned out to be a great listener. She never interrupted me once. She asked short questions that kept me talking. And she never made me feel stupid, like I was "overreacting," like I didn't know how to "take a joke." Also, she never told me to "just ignore them."

"Sexual harassment—and that's what this sounds like to me, Mila—is something I take very seriously," she said in a quiet, careful voice when I finally finished. "And not just because it happened to me, too."

"It *did*?" At first I thought I'd heard that wrong. Because, out of all the women I knew, Ms. Fender was probably the last one you'd pick to mess with. Well, except for Ms. Platt. And Ms. Wardak, who wore a whistle around her neck.

I stared at her, waiting for her to explain.

Then I couldn't look at her face at all. So I watched her hands in her lap: slender and beautiful, with bright pink nail polish, her fingers twisting in a way I'd never seen them do before.

I didn't want to hear. I mean, Ms. Fender was my *teacher*.

But I didn't want to *not* hear, either.

Our eyes met.

Ms. Fender was nodding. "Yes, it was several years ago, when I was student teaching. Not at this school," she added quickly. "It was a terrible experience, really just wrenching, but I did learn a lot about myself. And I know it can be different for different people, but I think it's never easy to talk about these things. You're a very strong person, Mila."

"I am?" My voice sounded as if it were coming from somewhere else in the room. Like suddenly I was a ventriloquist or something. "And you're not mad anymore? For how I wrecked the performance?"

She sighed. "I'd be lying if I told you I'm happy about it. We all worked so hard on that piece. I know you did too."

She'd noticed. Oh.

Ms. Fender reached over and patted my shoulder. Through my shirt, her fingers felt light and warm. "But I also understand that sometimes you reach a point where the only thing that matters is being heard. No, not just heard. *Listened to*, right?"

I breathed. "Right."

"I only wish you'd come to me before tonight, so we never had to get to this point, you know? But maybe some of that's on me. I was pretty tough on you when I changed your seat, wasn't I."

It was hard to know how to answer that. For a second I hesitated. Was she actually asking me to criticize her?

I decided she was. "It sort of seemed like you cared mostly about the solos. But also just how the band sounded. Not how I was feeling."

"I can understand why you thought so." Ms. Fender's

perfect eyebrows knitted together. "And I truly do apologize for that, Mila. You know, teachers see a lot, more than kids sometimes realize. But every once in a while something slips under our radar. And if I'd known any of this before today, I *promise* you I would have put an end to it. Can I ask you a question?" Her voice was gentle. "Have you told any of this to your mom?"

"Not really."

"Can I ask why?"

I wasn't going to explain about Dad, the checks he owed us, the fights on the phone. So I just said how Mom had lost her job, and how I hadn't wanted to give her more things to worry about.

"That's very considerate," Ms. Fender said. "But I think your mom needs to hear about it, don't you? And she's probably worried about you right now."

"She is?" I blinked.

"Well, after what happened onstage." Ms. Fender actually smiled a little then. "I'm sure by now someone's told her you're here, talking with me. Maybe she thinks you're in trouble."

I jumped up. "You're right, I should find her. But Ms. Fender?"

"Yes, Mila?"

"What will happen now? I mean, with the boys."

Ms. Fender folded her beautiful hands in her lap. "I

want to think about that overnight. Let's talk again tomorrow. Okay?"

"Okay. And thank you." Suddenly my voice quivered. "And . . . well, sorry about what I did onstage."

"I understand why you did it," Ms. Fender said. "I want you to know I support you, Mila. But I'm also glad you're sorry."

AFTER

That evening, when we got home, I went into Mom's bedroom, closed her door, and told her everything, just as I'd promised Ms. Fender.

At first Mom was calm, then furious. "Those boys—they had no right to treat you like that, sweetheart! And does Mr. McCabe know? I really think we should have another conference."

"No, no, don't call him," I begged. "Ms. Fender is taking care of everything."

"Are you sure? Because sometimes when a parent makes noise—"

"Please, please don't, Mom, okay? It's really important to me to do this with Ms. Fender."

"Okay. As long as this behavior ends." Mom's eyes

filled. "Oh, Mila, I'm so upset at myself. I should have realized—I mean, I knew *something* was going on, but I thought it was just regular middle-school stuff. With your friends."

"Well, it kind of turned into that," I admitted to her as we hugged. "But it's not your fault you didn't know; I basically kept it a secret from you. Because you had so much else going on."

"Oh, sweetheart, nothing is more important to me than you. *Nothing.* And can I say something? I'm really sorry your dad doesn't know you now. Because if he did, I'm sure he'd be very proud."

My throat ached. I didn't answer.

The truth was, I didn't know if I believed it. But it was good to hear her say that anyhow.

"As for those boys . . . ," Mom began.

"Yeah?" I asked, breathing in my Mom's shampoo. "What about them?"

She gave a jagged little laugh. "Hmm. Let's just say I'm glad you're back in karate."

Zara, Omi, Max, and Jared were waiting for me outside homeroom the next morning. When I saw them, my heart leaped into my throat. How much was I supposed to say about my talk with Ms. Fender? She hadn't sworn me to secrecy; but it seemed wrong not to keep it private.

And was this going to be another group discussion? Or another argument with Zara? Because with all the fireworks exploding in my head, there wasn't room for a single extra spark.

But right away the four of them surrounded me in a big, squeezy hug.

"Mila, you were awesome!" Zara shouted. "The way you took over the stage—"

"Did you hear us all cheering for you?" Omi asked.

"Well, but I was louder," Zara said. "FOR I AM THE LOUDEST."

"Excuse me," Ms. Wardak bellowed from across the hall. "Voices, please."

Voices, please, mouthed Zara as the hug broke up. I took a quick glance at her tee: WELCOME TO THIRST DAY OF YOUR LIFE.

Omi and I locked eyes. *You're the strongest biological creature,* she was telling me. *Small and tough, like a limpet shell.*

"Thank you," I told her aloud.

"But I didn't do anything," Omi said, blushing.

"Anyhow, Mila, it was really cool how you got back at Callum," Zara said. "Making him look stupid in front of everyone—"

"That's not what I meant," I said. "It's not why I did it, Zara."

"Well, that's definitely how it *looked*," Zara insisted. "Why *did* you do it, then?"

"Because I just . . . felt like I had no choice. But maybe that wasn't true. I talked to Ms. Fender about it, and . . . I feel bad about the whole thing, actually."

"Are you serious, Mila? The way the boys acted—"

"But maybe I didn't have to ruin the concert for everyone else. I don't know."

A weird pause.

"So what did Ms. Fender say?" Max pressed me. "Is Callum in trouble?"

"I'm not sure," I said. "She said we'll talk about it today."

"If you ask me, Callum should get suspended," Jared said. "Or expelled."

"*All* of them should," Max said, nodding. "Leo, Dante, Tobias—"

My stomach knotted. Was that the next step? It seemed pretty extreme, really.

Was it even what I wanted?

As angry and frustrated and hurt as I felt, as tired as I was of all the drama, I knew it wasn't.

CHOICE

Before I could even sit down in homeroom, I was told to go straight to see Ms. Fender.

"Mila, I have an idea," Ms. Fender announced as soon as I walked into the band room. "If it's okay with you, I'd like to arrange a community meeting."

"Com-mu-ni-ty mee-ting?" I repeated the syllables like I didn't trust them in my mouth.

"Oh, don't worry, not with the whole school! I just mean with the boys involved, and you, and whoever else you'd like to attend. Your choice, Mila. Could be a friend, or another teacher. And of course your guidance counselor."

"My guidance counselor had a baby. She's not here."

"Okay, well, someone else from the guidance department. And of course I'll be there to fully support you as well."

I swallowed a boulder. "I'm not sure. It just sounds so . . . *big*."

Ms. Fender reached across her desk to pat my hand. "I understand why it might sound that way, but I think it's crucial for the boys to understand that what they did isn't just personal; it actually affects *all* of us in this building. And this meeting will be an opportunity for them to hear your perspective, in your own words. With my *full support*," she repeated.

I tried to imagine what a "community meeting" would look like, but my brain had nothing.

And who would I even ask to come with me? Definitely not Zara. But maybe Samira? Or Omi? Or Max? Of course they'd say yes, if I asked, but they'd all seen *some* things, not *everything*. And what could they say that I couldn't say myself?

"I'm not sure," I admitted.

"You don't have to decide right this second," Ms. Fender said. "Or even today. But I do think the sooner we address this, the better."

I nodded. *Sooner the better.*

Ms. Fender smiled gently. "So will you let me know once you have a chance to think it over? It's fine to say no,

Mila, if you don't think it will be helpful. But I hope you'll trust me with this."

"Okay," I said. "I'll think about it."

I mean, I heard myself saying those words, but it didn't even sound like my own voice.

LIANA

Ever since the Tobias incident, I spent as little time as possible at the lockers. Not that I was expecting a repeat of the butt grabbing, but being in that hallway still gave me the jitters.

So at dismissal I opened my locker fast, grabbed my trumpet, my math textbook, and my best black pen, and stuffed my jacket into my backpack—all in one motion, no stopping. And I was just about to slam the door and run when I felt a soft poke in my right shoulder blade.

I jumped.

But it was just Liana.

"Oh," I said.

"Sorry," she said quickly. "I didn't mean to sneak up on you, Mila. I was just trying to get your attention. . . ."

"That's okay." I shut my locker door. "What's up?"

"Nothing. But can I please talk to you for a minute?" Liana's face was pale, her dark eyes were round and huge, and her mouth was turned down at the corners. Not the regular blank-on-purpose expression I expected from her.

And did she always have freckles? I'd never noticed them before.

She glanced over my shoulder at a bunch of boys down the hallway, laughing and shoving each other in a rowdy, end-of-school-day sort of way.

Our eyes met.

"Sure," I said. "Do you want to go somewhere?"

Somewhere else, I meant.

"Yeah," Liana said. "Maybe we can walk into town now? Unless you can't."

"No, I can. But I have karate this afternoon, so it can't be for long. One sec." I took out my phone and texted: **Hey mom. Need to talk to someone after school. Don't worry, everything fine. Can you pls pick me up in front of CVS in like 15 min & take me back to E Motions? Left my gi in the car yesterday so all set for karate! Thanks!!** I added a heart emoji.

Immediately Mom texted back. **Sure. Just be ready when I get there, bec I can't leave E Motions unattended!**

She added two heart emojis. I sent her three back.

261

Sometimes we had a kind of emoji war, but usually I surrendered pretty fast.

Liana and I walked a couple of blocks without saying very much. She slowed down in front of CVS, so I did too. And because I knew the clock was ticking, I blurted: "So what did you want to tell me? Because, not to rush this or anything, but—"

"Sorry! I'll be really fast, Mila. I just wanted to talk to you in private? About last summer?" She screwed up her forehead. "Some things happened to me in the town pool. Like maybe what happened to you."

"You mean . . . with the same boys?"

"No," Liana said carefully. "With Daniel and Luis. But Leo and Tobias were there sometimes, and I know they saw."

I didn't want to hear this. But I knew I had to. "What happened?"

"Okay." She took a shaky breath. "I was mother's-helping for this little girl who couldn't swim? So I was in the water with her a lot, and Daniel and Luis and this other boy I didn't know started playing this game. I mean, I *thought* it was a game. At first. But then it wasn't." She tugged her sleeves down over her hands. "They kept bothering me underwater. Blocking me so I was trapped, yanking my swimsuit. Saying things about how I looked in it. Laughing. And they wouldn't stop."

"Yeah, all that sounds familiar," I murmured. "Did you tell anyone?"

"You mean that stupid afternoon lifeguard?" Liana rolled her eyes. "He'd probably just think it was funny."

I didn't argue. I knew who she meant: a jokey dark-haired boy from the high school who never paid attention to anything in the pool. A couple of times I even spied him wearing earbuds, which was probably illegal. I mean, illegal for a lifeguard.

"What about the mom you were working for?" I asked.

"Yeah, I tried telling her. She said, 'Well, honey, you know I'm paying you to watch Skyler, not to interact with boys.' Like that's what you'd call it, *interacting*."

My phone buzzed. A text from Mom. **Ok, leaving E Motions. Pls be ready!!** Four heart emojis.

K. Five.

I slipped my phone in my pants pocket. "Liana, why are you telling me now? I mean, all this time—"

"Because I feel terrible about the band concert! And that I never said anything to you before that! Or stuck up for you! But I thought if I did, they'd just start bothering me all over again. I know it was selfish of me, Mila, and I'm really sorry!"

Her voice shook; either she was crying, or about to start. I threw my arms around her, and we hugged, which was awkward, because we were both wearing backpacks. Also, she was almost Zara's height, so I had to reach upward.

And that whole hug, it felt like a small tornado inside my head. All these emotions swirling around like crazy: I was relieved because it wasn't just me. Sorry for Liana. Angry that we'd both had this happen to us. Sad that it took so long to talk about it.

I also wanted to ask her a bunch of questions: Did what happened in the pool make her feel weird about her body? Or wonder if maybe she wasn't seeing herself right—or, anyway, like how the boys saw her? (If that even mattered? Because lately I was thinking it didn't.) Did things get tense and awkward with her friends, if she even told them? Did she tell *anyone*?

But there wasn't time for all these questions, not then. So I just asked the biggest one: how she got it to stop.

"I didn't," Liana admitted. "The summer basically just ended. And then when school started, it was like you were next."

"Yeah," I said, catching her eye. "For no reason. Just like there was no reason they picked you at the pool."

"I guess."

"No, seriously, Liana. *No reason.* And I wish you'd told me before, but I'm not mad at you or anything."

"Oh good! Because I was worried you might be. Although of course now the boys will just pick someone else."

"Maybe they won't."

"Ha," Liana said. "Right."

She deflated all of a sudden, like a popped balloon.

And that was when I made my decision about the community meeting.

And who I wanted to come with me.

FEELINGS

At the start of fourth period, Ms. Fender had arranged the chairs in a perfect circle. Nine chairs, at the far end of the band room, near the windows.

"Please sit wherever you like," she said, as if she'd invited us to a little-kid birthday party. So I pretended to pick a chair, knowing they were all the same anyway.

Liana sat next to me, her eyes round, her freckles sharp against her pale skin. Ms. Fender took the chair on my other side, smoothing her black skirt as she crossed her legs.

A small, dark-haired, young-looking woman I'd never seen before sat next to Liana.

"I hope it's okay that I'll be joining, Mila," she said in a friendly-but-not-too-friendly voice. "I'm Ms. Habibi, the maternity-leave replacement for your regular guidance counselor, Ms. Maniscalco. Ms. Fender has shared some of the details, so I think I'm pretty up-to-date. Unless there's something else you'd like me to know first?"

I shook my head. The saliva in my mouth tasted salty, like beach sand.

Also, my brain was spinning.

Good thing Ms. Habibi is here, because that means four females. Versus four basketball boys. So we're even!

Except there are five empty chairs. Why five?

Ms. Fender stood and took a few quick steps over to her desk. "Would anyone like some water?" she asked as she returned with her fancy pretend-marble bottle.

"No thank you," said Ms. Habibi. "But what a pretty bottle."

"Yes, it was a birthday present from my husband," Ms. Fender said politely.

Liana and I exchanged a look.

You can do this, her eyes said.

So can you, mine said back. *We both can.*

The door opened a crack.

"May I come in now?" a male voice asked.

As soon as I heard that voice, I knew who it was: Mr. Dolan, the guidance counselor. Who'd wanted to do the "friendly sit-down."

So maybe that's what this was—not a *community meeting*, but a *friendly sit-down*.

Well, I wasn't feeling friendly at all.

I broke out in an icy sweat. My shoulders felt tight, like they were attached to my body with strings that might snap any second.

"Yes, I think we're ready," Ms. Fender said. "Please come in."

Then she must have noticed my panic, because right away she turned to me and rested her warm fingers on my arm. "Mila, is it okay with you for Mr. Dolan to join us? You're in charge here, so please feel free to say no."

I sucked in some oxygen as Mr. Dolan crossed the room.

He stopped in front of my chair. "Mila, sorry I wasn't more helpful when you came to see me," he said in a quiet, serious voice. "I hope you'll let me stay; I really think this is something I need to hear. But if you're not completely comfortable, just say so, and I'll take off."

I caught Liana's eye. She nodded.

"Actually, I do think it's a good idea," I said. "If you listen."

"So do I," Liana murmured.

"Thank you," Mr. Dolan said. He took a seat in the empty-chair section.

Another soft knock on the door. And then in walked Leo, Callum, Tobias, and Dante. Not with their usual basketball-team energy: they were grim-faced and silent. Even their sneakers didn't squeak. And as they took the four empty seats, their eyes darted around the room (Callum, Dante) or stared at the floor (Leo, Tobias).

They're scared, I thought. And I almost felt sorry for them.

Almost.

"All right, I'd like to begin," Ms. Fender said. "Thank you all for coming. After what happened at the band concert, and learning *why* it happened, I thought we should meet as a community, because it really does affect us *as* a community. And I'd like Mila to use this time however she feels will be most helpful. It's entirely up to her. Is there anything you'd like to say first?"

She looked at me as if we were onstage, and she was the bandleader, giving me my cue.

Oh great, she's expecting a whole SPEECH?

My heart thumped. I shook my head.

Ms. Fender turned to Ms. Habibi, who smiled calmly.

"That's fine, Mila," Ms. Habibi said. "So if you think it may be helpful, we'd like to try a little exercise: we'd like to ask Mila to start a sentence with the words 'I felt' or 'I feel,' and to have each of you boys repeat it."

"Just repeat whatever she says? Word for word?" Dante made a face like he couldn't believe how kindergarten it sounded.

"Exactly," Ms. Fender said. "And that way we'll all know you've heard. And, I hope, listened." She raised her perfect eyebrows at me. "Want to give it a try?"

I shifted in the chair. To be honest, her idea sounded kind of dumb to me, too. But whatever. I didn't have a better suggestion for how to do this.

I took a shaky breath. "I feel really uncomfortable sitting here," I said.

"Sorry. Mila!" Ms. Fender got up quickly. "Would you like a different chair? I have a better one at my desk—"

"No, no. I mean, that's my sentence: I feel uncomfortable sitting here."

Ms. Fender smiled. "Oh, of course! Boys, now each of you, one by one, repeat Mila's sentence starting with 'Mila feels.'"

Mila feels uncomfortable sitting here.

Me: I feel sad that things got weird with my friends.

"All right, but what does that have to do with *us*?" Leo protested.

"A lot," I said. "And you're just supposed to repeat it, Leo."

"That's right," Mr. Dolan said, nodding at me.

Mila feels sad that things got weird with her friends.

Me: I felt angry when Callum made that joke before we went onstage.

Mila felt angry when Callum made that joke before we went onstage.

270

Me: I felt helpless when I heard about the scorecard. And humiliated.

Mila felt helpless when she heard about the scorecard. And humiliated.

Me: I felt weird when Leo tricked me into hugging him.

Mila felt weird when Leo tricked her into hugging him.

Me: I felt like crying when Tobias grabbed me by the lockers.

Mila felt like crying when Tobias grabbed her by the lockers.

Me: I felt annoyed when Dante sat too close in band, and on the bus.

Mila felt annoyed when Dante sat too close in band, and on the bus.

Me: I felt furious when Callum said I couldn't play untag. And that I should stop playing my trumpet—

"Okay, wait, Ms. Fender," Callum broke in. "I told Mila she couldn't play untag because we made a deal with Mr. McCabe, and I didn't want to get in trouble. And I only told her to stop playing trumpet that time because I was supposed to rehearse with you, and first I needed to warm up."

Ms. Habibi nodded at me. "Mila, would you like to respond? Up to you."

Me: I feel frustrated when Callum takes over.

Callum: Takes over *what*?

Me: Everything. This conversation. Space.

SWITCH

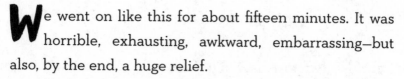

We went on like this for about fifteen minutes. It was horrible, exhausting, awkward, embarrassing—but also, by the end, a huge relief.

After I said everything I could think of, Ms. Habibi asked the boys if they wanted to speak.

"I do," Leo said right away. "I'm not saying it's an excuse or anything, but it was never personal. I mean, it was never really about *you*, Mila. I thought—we *all* thought—it was just fooling around."

"Well, but it wasn't," Tobias said in a choky voice. Suddenly his face crumpled, and he was crying. Ugly-crying, his shoulders shaking, snot streaming from his nose.

Ms. Habibi handed him a tissue from an invisible supply she must have been carrying in her pocket.

Liana and I exchanged a look. I could see she felt as squirmy as I did.

"*I* knew it was wrong, the whole time," Tobias said in between gasps. "I only did it because we were *all* doing it. And we were like a team, right? I mean, we *are* a team. And I thought if I said something, if I told you guys, 'Stop, leave Mila alone, I don't want to do this anymore,' you'd be like, 'Okay, fine, now you're off the team.'"

"You could have said something," Leo told Tobias. "We'd have listened to you."

I snorted. "Really? That's so funny, Leo. Because none of you ever listened to *me*."

"That's true," Liana said. "You didn't."

Dante's mouth twisted. "Well, we were wrong, then. I'm sorry we didn't listen, Mila."

"So am I," Callum murmured. His eyes met mine, then dropped to the floor.

We all sat there for a long minute, not saying much else. Tobias calmed down, but he still sniffled a few more times, so Ms. Habibi gave him another tissue. Finally she and Mr. Dolan left the room, and Ms. Fender told us to hurry to our lockers to get our instruments.

I couldn't believe it. Was Ms. Fender expecting us to have a band practice now? After everything we'd just said to each other? It seemed insane.

But we all got our instruments anyway. When we

had all sat down again, Ms. Fender asked me to play a random interval—a C followed by whatever other note I wanted. And then Liana and each of the boys had to hear what the interval was and play it back. We'd never done this before, and believe me, it was harder than it sounds. Although I guess it didn't surprise me that, of everyone, Callum was the best at it. Even when I was the most furious at him, I'd never stopped thinking he was great at music.

We did this repeating exercise over and over.

I didn't see the point of this part, to be honest.

And when we finished, Ms. Fender announced that she'd given it a lot of thought, and from now on she was making me leader of the trumpet section.

"*What?*" Callum's face went pale and his voice broke. "Ms. Fender, that isn't fair—"

"This isn't meant to punish you, Callum," she said quietly. "Although by now I think you understand my disappointment. It's really meant to recognize Mila's focus and hard work these past few weeks. Despite everything she's been sharing with us today."

I stared at my sneakers.

This whole class or meeting or whatever it was had me drained. Still, I was ecstatic. Leader of the trumpet section? Maybe this meant I was now Pet Number Three.

I knew I deserved it. I'd always been good at trumpet, and I'd been practicing extra hard.

But when I peeked at Callum, hunched over and silent, my insides felt weird.

After that was lunch. It was a chilly day with a sharp, stinging wind—not the kind of weather for being outside. Still, a bunch of kids were out on the blacktop, doing blacktop things.

As soon as I stepped outside, Max came running over.

"You okay?" he asked.

"Yeah, much better now." I didn't know I was going to say this, but it just came out. "And you were right."

"About what?"

"Talking about it. Telling people. And that time I said you didn't understand—"

Max held up a hand to cut me off. "Nah, forget it, Mila, we're good. You want to play untag? Jared and I are starting a game."

"Maybe later," I lied.

By then I'd spotted Callum sitting by himself on a bench, his hoodie zipped up to his chin, staring at his phone.

He's still upset about Ms. Fender's decision, I thought. So I went over to him.

"Hi," I said.

He looked up, startled. "Mila, we're not supposed to be within twenty feet of each other."

"I know. You going to report us to Ms. Wardak?"

He shut off his phone. "What do you want from me? I already apologized to you. And it won't happen again; at least, *I'll* never do it again. I don't know what else I can tell you, except the whole thing was like a stupid joke that came out wrong. And then it just kept going."

Callum's voice cracked. A strong wind ruffled his hair, and I watched him stuff his hands in the front pocket of his hoodie.

"I do that too," I said softly. "Say things that come out wrong. Actually, I do it all the time. But then I feel bad, and I try to fix it."

As soon as I said that, I thought: *And that's how I'm different from Dad.*

Now Callum was looking straight at me. "Yeah, well. I don't know if you can believe this, Mila, but we didn't *mean* to hurt you. We just didn't *get* it before. But now we do, okay?"

"Okay," I said.

"Anything else?" he asked, like he couldn't wait for this conversation to end.

I took a breath. "I just wanted to say I didn't know Ms. Fender would do that. Give me your chair, basically. I mean, she hadn't told me—"

"It doesn't matter."

"It doesn't?"

"Yeah. Because you'll be first trumpet if you deserve it. And if you don't, I'll get it back." Callum shrugged.

"Okay," I said again.

We looked at each other.

"But I don't think you will," I added, almost smiling.

BOW

The weeks sped by after that. All the bullying, or harassment, or whatever I was supposed to call it, had ended. After that conversation with Callum on the blacktop, I felt sure he would never do it again, and not Tobias, either. As for Leo and Dante, maybe they were truly sorry, or maybe Ms. Fender had just worn them out with all that repeating.

Muscle memory, or some sort of version of it, I guess.

Even so, there were other consequences. All four boys got three weeks of detention, and Mr. McCabe kicked them off the basketball team. They could rejoin it in the spring, he said, but only if they "demonstrated respect for the entire school community."

Also, Ms. Fender had them stand up in front of the

band and apologize for "unbandlike behavior." I apologized too, for wrecking the concert.

The week after the community meeting, Ms. Habibi and Mr. Dolan started a bunch of assemblies the whole seventh grade had to attend. They invited all these different speakers—some of them kids from the high school— to talk about Consent and Boundaries and Sexual Harassment. At first I thought it would be torture to sit there in the audience, but somehow it never was. Maybe because I was always surrounded by friends—Omi, Max, Jared, Samira, Annabel, Liana. And, about half the time, Zara too.

As Ms. Fender had announced, I was now trumpet section leader, totally focused on our next performance in December. This time I had a solo—not a big one, just four measures. But I was determined not to mess up, so I practiced like crazy.

Once, Callum even said I "crushed it." That was a huge compliment, coming from him, so of course I thanked him. He blushed, and after that we didn't say anything else to each other, even though he had the chair right next to me.

The other thing I practiced like crazy was karate. Because Mom was working at E Motions six days a week now, I never missed a class. Already I was getting ready for my yellow-belt test—and Ms. Platt said I was almost there.

But first I needed to work on my roundhouse kick, so she paired me with Samira.

One Saturday in late November, when I was working with Samira, I didn't notice who had just entered the dojo. All I saw from the corner of my eye was that someone had walked in wearing street clothes, and that Ms. Platt was speaking to him at the entrance.

And then suddenly Samira lowered her black pad. "Whoa! Ms. Brennan, stop."

"What's wrong?" I asked, thinking she was about to correct my kick.

"Nothing, you're fine," she murmured. "But see that boy who just came in? Who it *is*?" She squinted toward the door.

I turned my head and saw that it was Callum.

It was a funny thing. I knew I wasn't scared of him anymore, or angry, or confused, or any of those other feelings. But it was like my body hadn't learned what my brain knew, that I didn't need to worry about Callum Burley. And so my heart was banging when Ms. Platt walked over to us.

"Hey, Ms. Brennan, nice progress with those kicks," she said. "How about taking a short break to pair up with a potential new student? He says he wants to stay in shape for spring basketball, and he's here for some extra conditioning. But he's a complete newbie, so he'll need someone to talk him through the basics."

Samira and I traded a glance.

"You mean that boy over by the door?" I said slowly.

Ms. Platt smiled. "Yes. You know him?"

"Oh yeah, we definitely know him," Samira said. "Ms. Platt, maybe it's not such a great idea—"

"No, I'll do it," I interrupted. Ms. Platt had never paired me up with a new student before. It was progress for me to be asked.

And I couldn't be afraid of Callum anymore. I just *refused* to be.

But still, my stomach squeezed and my hands were damp as I followed Ms. Platt over to the door, where Callum was waiting. As soon as he saw me, he blushed a deep red.

"Oh, hi, Mila," he said.

"You need to call me Ms. Brennan," I replied, making my voice sound calmer than I felt. "I'll be calling you Mr. Burley. And lower-ranking students need to bow to higher ranks."

"You mean I need to *bow* to you?" he asked, like maybe I was joking. Or teasing.

"Exactly," I replied.

He did an awkward sort of bow, so I bowed correctly:

heels together, arms at my sides, eyes straight ahead, bending at the waist.

"Try it again," I said. "Try to follow what I just did."

He bowed again, better this time. I bowed back.

Callum smiled. Not a smirk, either—a shy little smile, like the sun peeking behind the clouds.

I couldn't help it; I smiled too. "You need to take off your shoes, Mr. Burley. Also your socks. And then follow me over to the mat, where we'll start with some stretches."

"Stretches?" He frowned. "Ugh. I hate stretches."

"Nobody likes them," I admitted. "But they're important, so we do them anyway."

I waited for Callum at the edge of the mat. He came over a minute later, walking unsurely, as if he didn't trust the floor.

It's really weird, but when you see someone's bare feet for the first time, they just seem so . . . helpless.

Then I peeked at his face. Our eyes met.

For some reason, he was doing his serious-musician expression.

I took a quick breath.

"Are you ready?" I asked him.

"Ready," he said.

"All right, Mr. Burley," I said loudly and crisply.

The second I heard myself, I thought it didn't even

sound like my own voice. Although the second after that, I thought: *Maybe it does.*

Maybe this is my actual voice.

"Please step onto the mat," I told him. "And now we can begin."

ACKNOWLEDGMENTS

Sometimes kids imagine writers sitting all alone, hunched in front of their computers with a cup of tea, waiting for inspiration. The truth is, many days are like that. But on many other days, writing is a team sport. So I'd like to thank the whole team behind this book: my excellent editor, Alyson Heller, and all the lovely people at Aladdin/S&S, especially Mara Anastas, Fiona Simpson, Tricia Lin, Michelle Leo, Chriscynethia Floyd, Chelsea Morgan, Sarah Woodruff, and Amy Beaudoin. Karen Sherman, thanks again for your eagle-eyed copyediting. Thanks also to Heather Palisi for the design and to Erika Pajarillo for the beautiful and bold cover art.

Jill Grinberg, you're the best agent out there. A deep bow to you and the whole agency—Denise Page, Katelyn Detweiler, Sophia Seidner, Sam Farkas.

Dr. Samantha Morrison, thank you for talking to me candidly about sexual harassment in middle school. I wish there were more professionals like you available to more kids.

A deep karate bow to the New Paltz Karate Academy for all they do to teach and inspire students. Special thanks to Maurey and Deena Levitz for sharing their expertise so generously.

Thanks to the #KidsNeedMentors program for connecting me with the classrooms of two amazing teachers, Corrina Allen and Gerilyn Lessing. And to their lucky students—the fifth graders at Minoa Elementary School in Minoa, New York, and the seventh graders at Bayshore Middle School in Bayshore, New York—thanks for helpful feedback and great conversation!

To my home team: thanks—again!—for endless love and support. Chris and Lizzy, bonus hugs for all those hours of reading and rereading! Josh, Alex, and Dani—thanks for always cheering me on.

ABOUT THE AUTHOR

Barbara Dee is the author of nine middle-grade novels published by Simon & Schuster, including *Everything I Know About You*, *Halfway Normal*, and *Star-Crossed*. Her books have received several starred reviews and been included on many best-of lists, including the ALA Rainbow List Top Ten, the Chicago Public Library Best of the Best, and the NCSS-CBC Notable Social Studies Trade Books for Young People. *Star-Crossed* was a Goodreads Choice Awards finalist, and *Halfway Normal* has been named to five state lists. Barbara lives with her family, including a naughty cat named Luna and a sweet rescue hound dog named Ripley, in Westchester County, New York.